THE BONANZA TRAIL

Dawson City was a rumbustious boom-town where whisky and champagne flowed. Men lost fortunes on the throw of a dice as thousands of greenhorns flocked into the Yukon's golden triangle. Hunter and guide Scope Mitchell was better equipped than most to survive the perils of the wilderness, but he had a battle on his hands when Frenchie Pete and his gang of thugs began stalking him. Would his lone rifle be a match for the outlaws?

JOHN DYSON

THE BONANZA TRAIL

Complete and Unabridged

LINFORD
Leicester

First published in Great Britain in 2006 by
Robert Hale Limited
London

First Linford Edition
published 2007
by arrangement with
Robert Hale Limited
London

British Library CIP Data

Dyson, John, *1937 –*
   The bonanza trail.—Large print ed.—
Linford western library
   1. Western stories
   2. Large type books
   I. Title
   823.9'14 [F]

ISBN 978–1–84617–623–4

Published by
F. A. Thorpe (Publishing)
Anstey, Leicestershire

Set by Words & Graphics Ltd.
Anstey, Leicestershire
Printed and bound in Great Britain by
T. J. International Ltd., Padstow, Cornwall

1

GOLD! GOLD! GOLD!

The heavy banner headline screamed out at him before he had even got off his horse. The latest copies of *The Seattle Post-Intelligencer* had been tossed by the stagecoach driver onto the stoop of the general store at Skykomish. From his saddle Scope Mitchell could read the sub-head:

Sixty-eight rich men back from Alaska.

The young rider, dressed in range clothes, stepped down and eased out a copy from the bundle. He tipped back his Stetson with a forefinger to reveal a slab of fawn hair and read the news.

Stacks of yellow metal arrives on the S.S Portland. Men bring out $5,000 to $100,000 each, ran another headline.

The shop bell dinged as Scope pushed inside, still reading avidly. He gave a whistle of awe. 'Hiya, Maud,' he yelled to the lady storekeeper. 'Sounds like there sure is some excitement down in See-addle.'

'How's that?' Maud snatched the copy from him. She, too, gave a low whistle through her gleaming dentures. 'Jeez! When this gets out there's gonna be excitement all over the US of A.'

Scope worked as a hunter and guide to tourists in the remote Glacier Peak region of inland Washington State but lately, thanks to a nationwide slump, he, like many others, had been finding it hard to make a living. Trophy hunters were few and far between that year of 1897.

The port of Seattle, on the north Pacific coast, was only 150 miles away so, as regards the rest of the country, he would be in with a head start. He glanced out of the window at his powerful Siberian husky, Kai, sitting patiently on the porch. Yes, with his dog team, and his ability to live off the land, he would have a distinct advantage.

'I've a damned good mind to go,' he said, as he pored over the story alongside Maud. 'Look at that!'

A photograph pictured a double row of Wells Fargo guards, shotguns raised across their chests, as a coffin-shaped box was carried down the *Portland's* gangplank. *Wells Fargo bring in $700,000 in nuggets and dust.*

'That's more cash than a body can imagine,' Maud moaned.

'Tell you what, ma'am,' Scope drawled, 'if you could fit me up with a decent grubstake I'd split with you half of what I bring back.'

'Huh: It says here one-way tickets on the *Portland* have already soared to two hundred and fifty bucks. Anybody fool enough to head for Alaska is gonna need a thousand or so for expenses, at least. That would be my life savings, young fella. Everything I possess apart from this ol' store. You think I'm crazy?'

'I'm going.' Like hundreds, soon thousands of young men across the country, Scope made a snap decision.

'With or without help.'

'It sure don't take long for a man to git gold fever. But if I was forty years younger I'd be goin' with ya, Scope. Lookee here!'

She fingered a picture of a young woman, Ethel Berry, *the bride of the Klondike*. While her husband, Clarence, panned for gold, the newly-wed Ethel had wandered about picking up nuggets lying on the ground including one weighing a pound, the biggest ever found. Between them they had brought back $130,000. 'No wonder she's smiling.'

Scope stroked his dropped jaw, wondering what he could do to raise some cash. Nobody, in these times, would want his cabin, and the horse would only raise thirty dollars. The one thing he had of real value was his hundred-dollar Marlin Ballard 10-shot repeating rifle, renowned for its amazing precision accuracy. And his Iver Johnson triple action revolver, the latest state of the art.

'I'd hate to sell my guns,' he muttered, 'but it looks like I'm gonna have to.'

'How you gonna survive without your guns?' Maud asked, her face concerned.

'All I'm gonna be needin' is a shovel and a pan,' he grinned. 'I'd better buy my supplies here 'fore I go rather than pay crazy prices in the frozen north.'

'It says here,' Maud piped up, 'that the best claims are going for five thousand dollars, that you'd be lucky to git one fer five hundred.'

'I'll find me one, doncha worry,' he called back, browsing around. 'Now, what am I gonna need? Flour, bacon, sugar, pinto beans, corn meal, baking powder, coffee, salt . . . I'd better make a list.'

'It says men need to traverse rivers and lakes to git to Dawson City. They need to take five-foot bullsaws, whip-saws, nails, pitch and oakum to build their own boats.'

'What's wrong with making a raft?

All I'll need is an axe, some wire or rope.'

'Even if you manage to git passage on a steamer they're gonna charge you extra for the dogs.'

'We'll git there,' he replied, stubbornly, 'even if I have to walk.' But he knew in his heart of hearts it would be virtually impossible to go by the land route up through Calgary and the Grande Prairies, far north to the Mackenzie River.

'Hot dang!' Maud exclaimed, opening her till and counting her cash. 'Did you mean that about goin' half-shares?'

'Sure I meant it.'

'Here y'are. Three hundred dollars. You call by in the mornin' after the bank's opened there'll be another six hundred waiting. You've cleaned me out, boy.' She shoved the cash across the counter. 'Any thang you need we'll put on credit, too. There's no fool like an old fool. But the best of luck, Scope.'

'Gee, thanks, Maud.' He stuck out his hand to shake hers with a hard squeeze. 'I'm sure gonna need some luck. That's the one thang a gold hunter does need. But, you'll see, I'll be back. We'll be rich.'

'Yes,' she sighed. 'All I can do is pray for that.'

★ ★ ★

'Mary, Mother of God!' Scope could hardly believe his eyes when he arrived at the dockside in Seattle. He had never seen so many folk congregated in one place. A seething mass of people packed shoulder to shoulder, 200 yards wide for a quarter of a mile, all trying to get onto one boat, *The Rosalie*, that was about to depart. The siren boomed, the single stack belched smoke, ropes were untied, hastily, and last-ditch attempts to jump aboard repelled, as *The Rosalie* moved out, packed to the gunwales.

Like all the others Scope watched her set off on the 1,000-mile trip along the treacherous coast. He stood hanging onto his horse, Rajah, who was heavily laden with sacks of flour, rolled oats, rifle, bacon, and so forth, plus his long-handled shovel, hammer-pick, bucket and gold pan. Kai, and his four other dogs, strung together, tongues lolling, looked similarly dismayed.

'What in tarnation we gonna do now, boys? Guess there ain't nuthin' for it but to join the queue.'

His dogs were an experienced team he had used in winter around the glacier peak. But he had left his sled at home as being too bulky to carry. What he would do for another he wasn't sure. It was July and winter in the Yukon would begin in September. He had a short summer to sort himself out.

Another problem was that tickets on *The Portland* had risen from $250 to $1,000 overnight. Daylight robbery, but he would just have to spend Maud's money unless he could find an alternative barque. Every available ship on the Pacific coast was being pushed into service: whalers, pleasure yachts, sailing sloops, cutters and ketches and

8

old rustbuckets that had been abandoned in Seattle's creeks.

So, Scope was in luck for one of the latter, *The Emma*, suddenly arrived dockside, her ancient engine clanking, pouring black smoke from her funnel, and instead of being last in the queue he was suddenly first. 'How much?' he yelled, as a gangplank was shoved out.

'Two-fifty for you and a hundred for the hoss,' a bearded sailor told him and waited palm of his hand outstretched as Scope found his cash. He braced his shoulders to hold back the excited crowd while he got on board with the dogs. Then he watched, anxiously, as Rajah, his legs flailing from a net, was swung aboard by a derrick.

He was not the only one with livestock for pigs, sheep, chickens in crates were being taken on. There were numerous mongrel dogs, too, brought along by men who had the mistaken idea they could be trained as sled teams, but which would be useless. While trying to prevent Kai from taking

9

these on in a snarling dogfight, Scope watched with interest the mass of humanity fighting to board.

The tenderfoot-type appeared to be in the majority, townies, some in silk shirts, others down-at-heel, who would have little idea how to survive in the wilderness. They hauled unwieldy, bulging baggage, tin stoves, tents, huge trunks. College boys, policemen, livery men, factory hands, cobblers, butchers, teamsters and barbers had arrived in Seattle from far and wide.

There were women, too, wives and sweethearts, if in the minority, one of them toting a sewing machine amid her baggage, another a newfangled, if cumbersome Remington typewriter.

What'n hell's she want that fer? Scope asked himself.

Their ship appeared to be an old collier, still grimed with black dust, and no attempt had been made to provide bunks for the passengers. They just had to find space on the floor in the hold not reserved for the animals. Scope took one look and decided to bed down on deck with his dogs. It would be cold and breezy, but what the hell! It would be better than that stinking hole.

'Excuse me, that space is reserved.' An authoritarian female voice addressed him and from where he sat he saw first of all a pair of black-laced bootees, an ankle-length grey dress, a tight-waisted jacket and, looking up, met a pair of serious grey eyes beneath a large hat.

'I ain't aware of any reservations on this ship.' Scope had found a spot behind the bridge which would hopefully protect him from the worst of the breeze. He didn't feel like budging but, being a gentlemen, he tipped a finger to his Stetson and grinned up at the pretty, oval-cheeked young lady. 'There's room fer me an' my dogs, ain't there?'

'Didn't you see my bag and coat? I've just been to get my other gear.' She held it in her arms as she frowned down at him.

From her well-spoken air, if not

11

downright snootiness, it seemed to Scope she must be one of those new, independent blue-stockings he had heard about. They were demanding all sorts of rights and there was a look in her eye which said, 'I'm your equal so stand up and give me your place.' It kinda put his back up.

'I allus had the idea that butts reserved seats, not bags,' he said, intending to annoy her. But, from the exasperated look on her face, he weakened and drawled, 'Make yourself at home, gal. We'll move along a bit.'

'Thank you.' There was a sharpness to her tone that quelled further intimacy as she went off to fetch other boxes and bags. *The Emma* was moving out before she was swamped by would-be gold hunters and, as the deck swayed the girl cried, 'Oh, my God!' and quickly sat down on deck beside him.

'Well, that was a bit of luck. Instead of being last we was first. Let's hope the luck holds.' He turned to the girl and stuck out his hand. 'Scope Mitchell. Pleased to meetcha, lady. You all on your own?'

'Yes, and that's the way I intend to remain,' she replied, tartly, but touched his horny hand with small, soft fingers, quickly withdrawing them as if they might get contaminated.

'I got a cabin up in the hills over there about a hundred and fifty miles inland.' Scope pointed to the fast-disappearing land mass behind Seattle. 'Where ya from?'

'New York.'

'New York? That's a helluva way away.'

'Not really these days. I travelled by the Central Pacific to San Francisco. Couldn't get a berth for love or money, so I took the stage up to here. Yes, I guess I was lucky, too.'

'So, from what you said just now, you ain't like them other gals on the look-out to marry a rich miner?'

'Perish the thought,' she replied. 'I wouldn't advise you to get any ideas

13

about me like that, yourself.'

'Lady,' Scope replied angrily, 'some woman is the last bit of extra baggage I need on this trip. An' I ain't rich yet.'

He tugged his hat down over his forehead against the stiff breeze, pulled up the collar of his fur-lined canvas coat, hugged Kai into him and stuck out his long legs in their heavy boots. 'Not at all,' he muttered.

Minutes of silence passed as they both stared out at the passing cliffs as the collier pushed up through Queen Charlotte Sound. Then the girl turned to him and said, 'I'm sorry, I didn't mean to be rude; it's just that I've got so tired of men trying to patronize me. My name's Alice Haskell. I intend to get to the goldfields under my own steam, work a claim and, hopefully, make a fortune.'

'Waal,' Scope drawled, 'I wish you good huntin'. But, to tell you the truth, lady, I don't think it's just gonna be a matter of picking up nuggets from the ground any more. Not by the look of

14

these crowds. We've both left it kinda late.'

'Courage,' she said. 'There's no room for pessimism. We're committed now.' She glanced at the rifle rolled in his tarp-covered sleeping pack. 'That's a vicious-looking implement. I hope you're not expecting trouble.'

'Nope. But I ain't plannin' on livin' solely on flapjacks an' beans. I'll be gittin' me some nice moose steaks.'

'You're probably better prepared for this adventure than most. At least, that's the feeling I get.'

'Maybe. An' I got the feelin' a good many of these idjits won't be making the return trip, millionaires or not.'

'You're being pessimistic again.'

'Lady, I'm lookin' at the facts. I hope I'm wrong.'

2

There were already twenty-five saloons going full blast in Skagway, a ram-shackle town of false-fronts and cabins hastily erected at the head of the creek where the would-be gold-panners disembarked. Discordant piano jangled out day and night, roulette wheels whirled, and the prospectors were fleeced of their cash before they had barely set foot in Alaska. The most notorious of these was Jeff's Place, run by a man better known as Soapy Smith.

Smith had been quick off the mark to abandon the diggings at Denver when he heard of the new strike. He had taken his gang of desperadoes with him. They had raised their boat fares from Seattle by their usual means, mugging men down dark alleys and holding-up stores. And they didn't intend to change their methods in Skagway.

In his white, high-crowned Stetson, gold-threaded waistcoat, striped pants, shiny boots, and diamond stickpin in his cravat, Soapy cut a foppish figure as he stood behind his plank bar and supervised activities in his crowded saloon. He had shipped in barrels of cheap whiskey and beer and recruited a bevy of down-on-their-luck girls who, in skimpy dresses, cavorted on a makeshift stage to the music, screaming and high-kicking in their version of the outrageous Parisian Can Can.

Their aim, of course, was to arouse the randy miners, lure them into curtained-off boxes around the room with promises of blissful kisses, and get their sticky-fingers on their pokes, which would be quickly passed through the curtains to accomplices.

Smith would have made a successful businessman if he was honest. But honest he was not. He had started out in life as a Texas cowhand, but poking longhorns was not to his taste. He had turned instead to street-corner thimble-rigging, inviting passers-by to find the pea under a walnut. He progressed from this to selling bars of soap, lucky customers were promised a thirty dollar bill inside one. The winning bar was always bought by his stooge in the crowd.

The trick had earned him his soubriquet, one which he hated. But the nickname Soapy stuck, maybe because of his blandiloquent southern drawl and oily manner of 'soaping' men up, as if butter wouldn't melt in his mouth.

Now in Jeff's Place the Wheel of Fortune was rigged, the cards marked, the liquor foul, the women fearsome and, if all else failed, a mark would be followed out into the street by his thugs, beaten to pulp, relieved of his cash and left to lie penniless and half-conscious in the mud.

Soapy couldn't lose. He was making so much money he didn't know what to do with it and scattered gold-dust about like confetti. At the same time, Smith had his sentimental side. He loved to be admired for his generosity. He started a widows-and-orphans fund for those left destitute, often as a result of his activities. And, like many maladjusted men, he could only have a loving relationship with a dog. He kept six, which he pampered and adored.

Why, he reasoned, as he stood outside his saloon and watched a ship called *The Emma* disgorging yet another flood of starry-eyed prospectors, would anyone want to face the perils of a winter in the Yukon with the far distant hope of finding gold? It was easier to make money staying put, relieving both those coming in and those going out, of their bounty. Law enforcement on this strip of Alaska was non-existent. True, it was prohibited to sell liquor, but who took any notice of that?

Later that night he was standing at the bar, his customary benign smile on his face, puffing at a cigar and chatting to his aide-de-camp, Frenchie Pete, when he noticed a tall young man step into the crowded, smoky saloon, accompanied by an attractive young woman. 'Who's this?' he asked. 'You seen him before?'

'No.' The scar-faced Frenchie shook his mop of black hair like a surly dog. 'Nor her.'

'You see that rifle he's carrying? What a beaut! I'd give two hundred dollars for that.' Smith smiled, soapily, at the stranger as he shouldered his way towards the bar. 'But I don't intend to.'

'She some looker, too,' Frenchie Pete slurred in his broken accent. 'She be OK in your troupe.'

'Yeah, I think we'll have 'em both, the gun and the girl.'

He polished a glass as Scope Mitchell confronted him. 'What's your poison, friend? We got the best whiskey on the beach. First drink on the house.'

When the SS *Emma* chugged up the creek to Skagway, Scope had been amazed to see that the beach was packed with people, thousands sitting on the boulders with their boxes and bundles, mainly men, of course. They had erected makeshift shelters of driftwood, tarpaulins, and tents, had built small cooking fires, and were ensconced on every available spare rock. Behind them stretched the township of plank cabins, stores and saloons.

'What they all waitin' fer?' he asked.

'They're waitin' to go over Chilcoot Pass,' a matelot said, as he helped lower a long boat and an anchor rattled down as the ship hove to. 'An' some of 'em have had enough and are waitin' to go home.'

Scope was concerned to see that it was a 200-yard haul to the beach by the longboat. 'How'm I gonna git my hoss ashore?' he asked.

'Well, you sure won't be rowin' him in the rowboat. Animals gotta swim, 'cept fer the pigs and chooks.'

Rajah was at that moment being hauled up from the hold in his net and deposited on deck as the passengers scrambled to get themselves and their belongings into the precarious longboat.

The seaman opened a gate in the rail. 'There y'are. He kin make it to the shore. The current ain't too strong. Give him a whack.'

'Hurry it up,' the captain bellowed from the bridge. He was in a hurry to get back to Seattle and pick up another fortune in paying passengers. 'Get that horse off the deck. We gotta catch the tide. It's on the turn and waits for no man. Unless you wanna come back with us?'

Scope caught hold of Alice's sleeve. He was reluctant to ask a favour but needs must. 'Can you see they put my bags on the rowboat and my rifle? Don't let 'em hang on to it for 'emselves.' He pulled off his boots and stuffed them into his sack, caught hold of Rajah and cinched his saddle tight.

'What about your dogs?' the girl screamed at him above the uproar.

Maybe he didn't hear her, for he was already in the saddle, pulling on the reins to spin the horse in an arc on the slippery deck as folks scrambled to escape the flying hoofs. Scope kicked his heels hard into his sides, twisted the gelding's ear, making him whinny and prance, and urged him towards the edge. With a flying leap they were away, hitting the icy water hard.

Scope gasped with the shock, but Rajah's head was coming up, and he hung on, aiming him towards the shore. He turned in the saddle, gave a piercing whistle and Kai hurled himself from the deck into the briny and was swimming furiously after him. The other dogs were more reluctant, but the sailor kicked them on their way, and they were soon all doggy-paddling plaintively strung out in the wake.

The tide was turning and it was a hard struggle but Scope urged them all on and Rajah was broad of beam and a good swimmer. Eventually they waded ashore and Scope jumped off and turned to greet his dogs as they splashed and shook themselves. One of the rowboats was returning. It looked like Alice would be on the next one to arrive.

'Whoo!' His teeth were chattering

from the cold. 'This ain't a good start.'

He loose-hitched Rajah to a rock and clambered along the beach to retrieve his gear as the longboat came in. Then he helped Alice out with her several packs. 'There's a spare spot up back of the beach under them pines. I'm gonna make me a fire an' dry out,' he said, between judders of cold. 'You wanna jine me, or what?'

'OK,' the girl replied, wringing the water from the bottom of her skirt. 'I'll bring my stuff up.'

Most men had so much by way of equipment and supplies they couldn't move it in one go and had to make two or three portage trips. It took time. Most had a partner to make it easier, but Scope wasn't sure what he was going to do. Having a woman along was likely to be more of a hindrance than a help.

However, at that moment he was more interested in finding dry, dead kindling to get a blaze going and his coffee pot on. By the time Alice had struggled up the beach with the last of her equipment he had wrapped a blanket around his waist, had stripped off his sodden check shirt and long-sleeved flannel vest and was briskly towelling his hair. He squeezed out his soaking long johns, socks and corduroy pants and hung them on sticks to dry. 'Excuse my nakedness,' he said.

Alice glanced at him, but whether she was taking in the sight of his willowy, high-shouldered physique, the lean muscles like whipcord from days spent in the saddle, he wasn't sure. Maybe she was more interested in the money belt around his narrow waist containing Maud's cache of twenty-dollar gold pieces, or what was left of them after paying his fare.

'Never trust a woman, especially a young, pretty one,' had become his maxim after some bitter experiences. But maybe he should give her the benefit of the doubt.

When he had rummaged in his pack

for his set of spare underwear and shirt, filled a tin mug with scalding coffee, shared it with her and warmed himself at the blaze, he was feeling better prepared for the rigours facing them. 'First, I'm gonna try find a man who looks like he knows the score and hear tell what's up ahead. Best place for that's the saloon. I could do with a whiskey-warmer, too. You comin'?'

'I don't know. There appear to be some cabins advertising beds. I could do with some rest before I start.' She was fussing about, sorting out her belongings. 'I may have to abandon some of this stuff. I'll have to find an Indian porter to help.'

The Chilcoot Indians were, indeed, offering their sturdy bodies to carry packs to the top of the pass. For a while they had watched in wonderment when the first of the gold-rushers arrived on this barren, windswept bay. What did they want? Where were they all going? At first they had been hostile. Already the white hunters had slaughtered their sea otters almost to extinction. Then they had started on the seal colonies. Perhaps they were now intent on taking their salmon, the Indians main source of livelihood, or their bears? When they discovered it was just the worthless, sparkling yellow pebbles the whites coveted they had become more friendly. They were welcome to them. What good were they to anyone?

Paid for their services with white man's dollars, the Chilcoots had discovered they could buy useful utensils. And the fiery water that made a man laugh and feel good and fall over. Sometimes fight and kill. Whiskey! Some braves had developed a terrible thirst for it.

'Please yourself,' Scope drawled, combing back his thick, fawn hair, sticking his Stetson on top, pulling on his boots and picking up his rifle. 'I'm gonna take a look at the town.'

He asked his nearest neighbour to keep an eye on his horse, dogs and gear and strode away along the beach. 'Wait a minute,' Alice Haskell called, putting on her hat. 'I *will* come with you.'

'What'n hell time is it, anyhow?' Scope remembered that as you got near the land of the midnight sun there would only be about four twilight hours to mark the night in summer times. 'It's gonna take a bit of adjusting to.'

'Ten-thirty. Yes, it is odd. Most people would be in bed by now at home.'

'Seems like all the world's arrived at Skagway.' In fact, there were now 30,000 people herded together in this 'town' that had been non-existent a year before. Japanese, Chinese, Russians, Mexicans, Peruvians, Irish, French, German. 'What a weird crowd. What a babble of tongues. Don't nobody speak American?'

Most of the saloons and eating houses were jam-packed but the biggest and liveliest seemed to be Jeff's Place. Scope stepped up on to the wooden sidewalk and called, 'Come on.'

Alice appeared hesitant. 'You're not going to get drunk, are you?'

'Who knows?' He grinned and pushed into what at first seemed bedlam. Through a canopy of tobacco smoke and the flickering flames of whale oil lamps he saw men crowded three-deep at the bars. Others were packed around the roulette table intent on other games of chance. Some were gawping up at screaming dancing girls on a stage, who were kicking up stockinged legs in rustling scarlet satin dresses and flailing petticoats. 'Waal, I'll be doggoned,' Scope drawled. 'A veritable Sodom and Gomorrah.'

Other men, crammed into available spaces around the walls, sat on empty barrels, drinking, smoking and talking, or shouting at the top of their lungs. 'Grab a couple of those seats, gal. What you havin'?'

'Something non-intoxicating,' Alice cried.

A pudgy gent in a tall white Stetson, and otherwise flamboyantly attired, presided at the bar amid his lackeys. 'What's the lovely lady's tipple?' he asked. 'She your bride?'

'No she ain't. Just a friend.' Scope gave a frown, wondering what business it was of this character's. 'Gimme one of them sarsasparillas.'

Soapy Smith took his time pouring it, then offered his clammy hand. 'Might I introduce myself? Jefferson Smith, the Robin Hood of the frontier. I run this joint and, I might add, most of the town. Anything I can do for you and the lady just let me know. You headed up the pass?'

'I ain't sure yet.' Scope pulled his hand away and wiped it on his pants. 'But that's my business, ain't it?'

'Hech!' A burly, greasy-looking Frenchman, leaning on the bar, gave a deep-throated chuckle. 'You a real friendly *hombre*, huh?'

He slapped Scope's shoulder. 'That no way to be. Soapy just geev you free drink. You not grateful?'

'Forget it, Pete,' Smith said. 'You're welcome, stranger.'

'You're spilling my drinks, pal,' Scope drawled, easing out of the middle-aged

Pete's embrace and making his way back to Alice.

She was perched on a barrel giving an icy smile to some gnarled old-timer who was ardently haranguing her.

'Move over, mister,' Scope said, squeezing between them. 'What did he want?'

'He offered me two thousand dollars to marry him. Most insistent. He says he's got a claim up at Eldorado Creek.' She watched the prospector weave his way towards the bar. 'How curious.'

'So what did you say?'

'I had to reluctantly decline.'

'Don't worry. There'll be other offers. Wimmin are at a premium up here. Maybe you should hold out for half-a-million.'

She sipped at her sarsasparilla and remarked, 'You haven't got a very high opinion of the feminine gender, have you?'

Scope leaned his rifle against the wall and stuck out his long legs, taking a swallow of the coffin varnish. In between trying not to choke on its high-octane velocity, he muttered, 'I don't have that high an opinion of mankind, generally. That slimy varmint behind the bar is no exception. Soapy Smith. I've heard of him from some place, and it ain't good.'

'Why do they call you Scope?' she asked.

'It's just a nickname that stuck. I used to experiment with a 'scope on a rifle but it was too dang heavy and didn't improve my shooting much. What did you do in New York, Alice?'

'Oh,' she replied, airily. 'Nothing much that would interest you.'

'So, you're a bit of a mystery, huh.' He turned and met her grey eyes, smiling at her, touching her chin with his pointed finger as if he would like to kiss her . . .

But she jerked her head away. 'It's nothing I wish to talk about, that's all.'

'Like that, is it?' he muttered and noted that Smith was pushing his way through the crowd towards them.

'Some of them dancin' gals don't seem to have no knickers on,' he said, to change the subject.

'Yes, I had noticed that. What a debauched and depraved place to take a lady.' But she gave a little giggle as if it was all rather amusing. 'Who's this?'

'A slug crawled out from under a stone, otherwise known as Soapy Smith.'

'Howdy.' Smith bowed, flamboyantly, and grabbed Alice's hand to raise to his lips. 'What an enchanting creature. Randolph Jefferson Smith at your service, milady.'

He waved a scruffy prospector out of the way and took a seat beside her. 'Are you headin' for the Yukon? I should warn you there are formidable hurdles. First you must get along the creek to Dyea, then attempt the more or less vertical climb up the pass to the glacier. In winter its ice and in summer slippery mud and, as you can guess, packed with these scum of the earth. At the top you'll find the Mounties waiting for you for you'll be entering the Dominion.'

'Mounties?' Scope echoed.

'Yes, North West Mounted Police. They have a post at the border.' Soapy put out his hand towards Scope's rifle. 'They impose a tax on all goods going through. This fine weapon, for sure, will cost you twenty-five dollars import duty.'

'Twenty-five dollars!'

'At least. More for your ammunition. May I look at it?'

'Sure, why not?' Scope shrugged. 'It's a Marlin Ballard.'

'Not *the* Marlin Ballard.' Smith picked up the rifle with awe. 'I've read about this but this is the first time I've — '

'Solid top receiver and side ejection. Won't git no snow in there to choke up the works.' There was a note of pride in Scope's voice. 'Same rifle as used by Annie Oakley for her fancy shootin'.'

'No!' Soapy gasped. 'I remember reading that at trials they got all ten shots in the centre of the bull at two hundred yards.'

'Careful,' Scope warned as Soapy touched

the trigger. 'There's one up the spout.'

'Don't worry, I'm an expert shot, as no doubt you are, too, er . . . what was the handle? Scope?'

'That's me,' Scope said.

'How much would you want for this?'

'It ain't for sale. They started making 'em in '89 and ceased in '95. They're hard to git hold of.'

'Yes, I dare say,' Soapy remarked, replacing it against the wall.

'Guess I'll git me another whiskey. You want another, Alice?'

'No, this one's made me whoozy. Thought you said it was non-alcoholic.'

'Aw, it's just the heat in here, thassall. How about you, Smith?'

'Sure. I never drink the house whiskey. Bourbon's my tipple. Ask them for my special glass.'

As soon as Scope headed for the bar Soapy's hand squeezed Alice's knee. He was pleased to see that the gin he had slipped into her drink was having effect. 'Are you two travelling together?'

'Not really.' She caught hold of his

hand to prevent its progress up her thigh. 'Please don't do that.' She picked up the hand and tossed it away as if it might be a rancid piece of meat.

But Soapy was not subdued. 'Fifty folk were buried in an avalanche on that pass last month. This is the weather for it. Frostbite, mosquitoes, Indians, God knows what you're going to have to face. Why don't you stay here and work for *me*.'

'Oh, yes,' she sighed. 'What as?'

'My secretary. Money for old rope. I like you, sweetheart.' Soapy made sure that Scope's back was turned to them, nudged her with his knee and put his mouth to Alice's ear, whispering to her.

She jerked her head away. 'How foul! Leave me alone, will you?'

Whatever he had suggested, Smith smirked, and got to his feet. 'You'll be back, sister, and maybe you won't be so hoity-toity next time. I'm making you a good offer. Take it while you can.'

He turned, accepted his glass of bourbon as Scope returned, and moved away through the tables the tumbler of whiskey in his hand.

'What's going on? You feel all right?'

'Yes, I'm just a bit dizzy, that's all. I'll be OK once I'm outside. I'm going back to the beach. You stay here.'

'Hang on, I'll come — ' But Alice was already moving away, reaching the door. 'Must admit it does stink to high heaven in here.'

He didn't feel too good himself after he had knocked back another mug of the hard stuff. His knees were weak and his head spinning as he fumbled to pick up his rifle and make for the exit. When he got outside he noticed an alley up the side and decided to take a leak. He was standing there, tucking himself away, when he heard a movement, and the next he knew a heavy implement thudded into the side of his head. He stumbled aside, knocking over the rifle, and glimpsed Frenchie Pete, a blackjack in his fist, swinging it for another blow.

Scope raised an arm and warded him off, but was immediately held from behind by another assailant, who pulled his arms back and Frenchie let him have it across the other side of his head.

Scope swung up his boots and kicked Pete in the face. He saw him snarl and tumble back. He leaned forward to send the other thug rolling over him to land on top of his accomplice in a crumpled heap.

But there were others. A shadowy figure came in, hacking a cudgel at his knees. 'Ouch!' Scope cried, caught hold of the man's wrist, pulled him forwards and gave him a straight right to the jaw.

He turned to another, who had a knife at the ready. 'So, it's like that, is it?' He felt for his belt and pulled out his own Bowie, razor sharp. 'Come on, pal. I'll cut your heart out.'

The others were struggling to their feet and, cudgels, knives and chains at the ready, they circled around, swinging at him, closing in. 'You're a dead man, mister,' Frenchie snarled.

As Scope backed away along the alley they suddenly heard a female voice ring out. 'Not so fast!'

The five mug-hunters turned and saw Alice standing there, the rifle in her hands. 'Leave him alone!' She fired, the explosion cracking out, making them all jump. The bullet whistled past Frenchie's head. 'That was just a warning. The next is for real,' she gritted out, as she levered the Ballard. 'You had better get back into that rathole where you belong.' She indicated the side door of the saloon. 'Go on! Skat!'

'Hey,' Scope breathed out, as he watched them scuttle off, and wiped the trickle of blood from his face. 'That was some shootin'.'

'Are you all right?' she asked.

'Sure.' He forced a smile. 'You better give me that back now 'fore you kill someone.'

'To tell the truth, I didn't mean to press the trigger. So it's lucky I didn't hit anyone.'

'C'mon. We better git outa here.' He picked up his hat. 'Thanks for saving my bacon, anyway.'

3

Chilcoot Pass was a sight to behold. A never-ending line of mainly black-clothed men was edging its way like a slow-moving caterpillar up the almost vertical slope of the Chilcoot Pass towards the glacier. Beyond, the icy fangs of the northern Rockies towered over them. Frequently the chain would come to a halt as somebody lost their footing, or their load. Or there was some other hold-up.

'There's no way I'm going up there, not with my hoss and my dogs,' Scope said. For a start he did not relish paying exorbitant taxes to the British Dominion. He took a look at an alternative route, White Pass, but the brutal treatment to the pack animals who were being whipped up the slope horrified him. There was no fodder for the horses and, once they were worn to a frazzle they were left to limp about until they collapsed in the mud and starved to death. Thirdly, he had heard of another, a little-used overland route he intended to try.

'I guess I just ain't got the herd instinct,' he told Alice, after giving her a hand with her bundles along the valley to the foot of the Chilcoot climb. 'I've never been inclined to follow where too many other men go. But you should make it OK, gal.'

What was that look in her eyes as she swivelled her head back towards him? Was it fear of abandonment? But she pressed her lips together, frowned and cried, 'That's OK. Thanks for your help. You go the way you think best. Good luck.'

'So long,' Scope called, turning his horse. 'Maybe we'll meet again.'

He felt a bit of a louse leaving her. She was, he knew, too proud to ask him to take her with him. Too independent. But how could he carry her and her boxes with him? Rajah and the dogs

41

would have to struggle to carry his own baggage.

She's a spunky gal, he told himself. She'll make out and there's plenty of fellas on that trail'll be glad to help her.

There had also been a sudden influx of other women: 350 of them had sailed from New York on the *City of Columbia* to make the 16,700-mile trip by way of Cape Horn. Some planned to take out miners' certificates and scoop up nuggets themselves. Others had business projects in mind. There were plenty of ways to make cash by opening boarding-houses, restaurants, bakeries. One said she planned to start a brokerage business. So Alice would have plenty to chat about.

Most men were carrying huge 500 lb loads of flour, sides of bacon, 100 lb tins of dried fruits, sacks of beans, 36 lb cakes of yeast, and so forth, which they hoped would see them through the winter. Fair enough, but Scope preferred to travel light and try to live off the land. Some of the women had stacks of extras like tins of cookies, cakes, pickles, butter, bars of castile soap and other toiletries. Some carried wash basins, eiderdowns and pillows, while one had a hand-painted lamp complete with shade. This seemed to be going a bit too far.

However, he had no call to feel smug. He could well be in trouble himself. Anybody could be, out alone in that kind of country, especially when sub-zero winter blizzards set in.

He rode back past the plodding stream of hopefuls to Skagway and, before picking up his load, stepped down outside the saloon called Jeff's Place. He left his rifle rolled in his blanket, but he had taken the precaution this time of buckling on his gunbelt with the Iver Johnson snugly in its holster on his hip.

It was still early morning and Soapy was sitting on a bar stool in a green eyeshade weighing gold dust on the scales and counting the take in dollar bills and coins from the previous night's activities. He looked for all the world like a vicious startled rat as he suddenly saw Scope heading towards him.

'Howdy,' he called, recovering himself, but giving the bar-keep a nudge with his elbow. 'Thought you'd have been on your way by now. How can I help you?'

'You mean you thought you'd have been in possession of my rifle and wallet.' Scope placed his fists on the edge of the bar and stared at him, aggressively. He caught sight of the 'keep backing away then groping for something under the bar. 'You can leave that shotgun where it is, mister. You better bring your hands up empty, or else.'

'What 'n hell's got into you?' Soapy asked.

'Don't try to act the innocent with me, Smith. You know what's gotten into me.' Scope pointed to the bloody bruise on the side of his forehead. 'Your bully boys thought they could beat me senseless. Well, they got a surprise, didn't they?'

44

'What on earth are you talking about? My bully boys? If anybody attacked you it was nothing to do with me. I deplore violence of any kind.'

'Shut your lies, you slimy toad.' Scope grabbed him by his shirt front and dragged him across the bar. 'I know what tricks you're up to. How many other poor devils have you robbed?'

'I protest.' Smith flailed his arms trying to take a swipe at Scope. 'Let me be. You'll regret this.'

Scope slapped him hard across his face and back again making the saloon owner's teeth rattle. 'Where's your pal, Frenchie Pete, today? I've got a bone to pick with him.'

'He's not here,' Soapy spluttered. 'He's gone.'

'Yeah, I bet he has.' The young hunter hurled the saloon owner back to go crashing against his shelf of glasses. 'You just give him a message from me and understand this yourself. Next time it won't be fists against blackjacks and chains: it will be this.' He pulled the triple action and crashed shots into bottles above and around Smith, who cowered back, his hands protecting his face. 'You get the message?'

This time the bar-keep did come up with a sawn-off, but Scope was too quick for him and blasted the weapon from his hands. The man screamed and shook his blood-shattered fingers.

'You'll have to do your shootin' left-handed from here on, buddy.' Scope backed away as Soapy got to his feet, scowling at him. 'You picked the wrong man to try jumping,' he said.

'We'll get you,' Smith howled, pointing a finger at him. 'Nobody does that to me. We'll get you, and that stuck-up bitch of yours. You've got to come back this way.'

'Sure, you frighten me.' Scope turned on his bootheel and stepped outside to his horse, swinging aboard and clipping away down the muddy street. Well, he grinned to himself. I feel better for that.

★ ★ ★

Frenchie Pete was not the usual common or garden enforcer. He had a history, one that had turned him into a very bitter man, even a laughing stock on the Alaskan coast.

He had started out in life as a *voyageur*, a trapper, making intrepid journeys with his companions into the wilderness, so he, too, knew how to live off the land. But he had sought a more sedentary existence and had opened a log cabin store in the small port of Sitka on the coast.

It was in 1880 that a couple of prospectors, Joe Juneau and Dick Harris, first hit it rich, so Pete had set off with his squaw in his small skiff to take a look at Gold Creek. A storm had blown up and they had been wrecked on Douglas Island so Pete was forced to dig in for the winter and wait for rescue.

He took his pick-axe to a cliff and soon found traces of gold. But it was poor stuff and embedded deep in the rock. Pete was not a man fond of hard work and by the time he had got back to Sitka in the spring he only had a couple of hundred dollars'-worth of the sparkly stuff. So he went back to running his store.

It so happened a man named John Treadwell had arrived in Sitka. An experienced mining engineer, he offered to go over to the island and take a look at Pete's 'Paris Lode'. He returned with samples of lowgrade ore and offered to take over the mine.

Frenchie Pete readily agreed and signed an entry in the Book of Deeds of the district recorder: 'Transfer of Paris Lode from Pierre Erussard (or Frenchie Pete) original locator to John Treadwell in consideration of the sum of five dollars.'

Treadwell had started with five stamp mills. Now, eighteen years later there were 880 operating and the Alaska Treadwell mine was the largest gold mill in the world.

In Jeff's Place that morning, after his run in with Scope, Soapy was reading a copy of the *Alaska Packet* and when Frenchie Pete strolled in, drawled, 'Waal, whadda ya know, here comes the mighta-been millionaire. I see Treadwell's just turned down sixteen million dollars for your mine.'

'Very funny,' Frenchie growled, as the doxies sitting around on the battered sofas before business began giggled with mirth. Of course, no single panhandler could have made much impression on that hard-rock mine, but he was sick of the ribbing. It accentuated his sense of being ill-done by the world. Angry bile surged up in him and he spat in a spittoon, spat out his hatred. 'I'll make me some more gold one day. Then you'll laugh!'

'Sure,' Soapy smiled, winking at the girls. 'But it won't be by digging for it.'

Pete got stuck into a bottle of whiskey and scowled at them, taking his blackjack from his pocket and slapping it on his palm. 'This is as good a tool as any trade.'

'Exactly my idea, my friend. I have an

assignment for you.'

'Yeah, just what would that be?'

Smith lowered his voice. 'That young stranger was in here again. He's vowed to settle with you. I want you to follow him. Watch and wait. He seems the sort who might strike it lucky.'

Frenchie Pete took a slurp of the whiskey, shook his hairy head like a sullen mastiff and swivelled his muddy eyes. 'So?'

'So, that's when you strike. You get that rifle, that revolver. I want them and I want him dead. You can keep his gold.'

'Boss,' Pete growled, sticking out his paw, 'you got a deal.'

'Take four of the boys but try not to let him know you're on his trail. Savvy?'

'Sure, he won't get back to Skagway alive.'

'Good,' Soapy said, glad that Frenchie Pete would do his dirty work for him. 'I'll meet you up in Klondike City in a month. I'll bring the rest of the gang. It's time we took over up there.'

'It'll be a done thing by then,' Pete assured him. 'He won't get away a second time.'

'Good. And keep an eye out for that feisty gal. A good looker like her needs to be capitalized on,' Soapy grinned. 'Know what I mean?'

★ ★ ★

Another of the old-time prospectors, Joe Juneau, was fifty-two when he made his big strike. He had for a while been a wealthy man, lived like a lord, spending his cash, treating his friends to his largesse: crates of imported champagne, Havana cigars, and the favours of willing women. Eventually all his cash had slipped through his fingers and his friends had gone.

'You want to find out about the chances of finding gold up there,' a storekeeper told Scope Mitchell, who had been asking around for information, 'you wanna go talk to Joe Juneau.'

He found him, a hunch-backed old

man of seventy, making a sort of living along the shore helping to land the goods and livestock of the never-ceasing flood of bonanza-seekers.

Scope knew the best way to loosen the tongue of an old bum like Juneau was to offer to buy him a bottle in a saloon.

'I'm too damn old to go prospectin',' Joe muttered, 'much as I'd like to be your partner, young fella.'

'That's a pity. Couldn't you give me any idea which is the best creek to try?'

Old Joe took another bite out of the bottle and peered at him through rheumy eyes that had seen too many blizzards in their time. 'At least they named the town of Juneau after me,' he cackled.

'Yeah, big deal.' It looked to Scope like he was wasting his time with this character. He got up to leave and pressed a five dollar gold piece into Juneau's hand. 'Buy yourself another bottle, old-timer.'

'Hang on,' Joe called out, testing the

coin with his last few teeth. He dug a rumpled claim form from his pocket. 'You won't find a spare claim up on any of them creeks by now, not after this stampede. This here's one I took out on Hunker Creek off the Klondike River. I been meanin' to go back there. I guarantee there's gold, but it's deep. You'd have to dig down at least ten feet. You can have it for five hundred dollars.'

Scope looked dubiously at the tattered form, but it seemed to be official, registered at the Mounted Police post in Dawson. He knew, though, that many a tenderfoot had been skinned by these sort of phoney claims.

'I dunno,' he pondered, taking a sup of the whiskey, himself. 'I only got three hundred dollars to spare. Tell you what, I'll give you two hundred for this.'

'Aw, hell, why not,' Juneau yelled, as Scope dug deep for his money belt. 'Go for it, boy. And, remember, you hit it rich I want a quarter share.'

'Yeah, sure,' Scope replied, reluctantly parting with the cash. 'I must be crazy, but I'll give it a try.'

4

It was good to get away from the knee-deep mud and the ripe stench of humanity, the crowds pouring into Skagway. Good to be out on his own, riding Rajah, dragging his pack on a travois, Indian-style, to breathe in clean air and feel the breeze on his face. Kai and the other dogs trotted along behind, each carrying a 30 lb bundle across their shoulders, their tails wagging to show they, too, were glad to be on the move.

The route Scope had chosen was known as Jack Dalton's trail, which had been used to march animals through to Fort Selkirk. It started behind Pyramid Harbour and followed the Chilcoot River for a winding forty miles or so until it started the ascent to the 3,000 ft. high divide. It was a trail not much used because, as men said, there was 'too much walking': in all, 350 miles of it.

But the sun was shining, the scenery magnificent, the mountainsides swathed with dark pines, masses of wild flowers in bloom along the river's banks, and the water babbled merrily by. Scope whistled a popular air as Rajah picked his way through the rocks. This was the life. His grip tightened on his rifle when he sighted bears, but they were too busy filling their bellies with summer berries to pay him much heed.

There were blueberries, wild cherries, cranberries, raspberries and bilberries in masses on the bushes and Scope helped himself to mouthfuls because he figured if they kept the bears so strong and healthy, the Indians, too, they should be good for him.

The first night he built himself a half-bivouac shelter, with a raised platform for a bed of pine needles, cutting the boughs quickly and economically. He made a rock fireplace over which his billycan was suspended by a panhook of greenwood. He baited his line and soon had a dozen trout sizzling over the embers. He tossed most to the dogs and devoured two himself. There was plenty of grass for the horse to graze so he hobbled him nearby and listened to him munching as he lay back on his goose-feather bag and lit his pipe to keep the 'skeeters at bay.

The latter were one of the biggest problems in the Yukon. On the marshy ground there could be unending clouds of them and it had even been known for them to blind a bear by their fierce stings until it stumbled around, bellowing its agony, and drowned in the swamp.

But Scope had come prepared with a mosquito net which he draped over his bivouac and retired behind intent on resting his weary limbs during the short night. The other problem was the possibility of bears raiding the camp, but once he had cleared away the remains of their meal there was little to attract them. Nonetheless, he slept with the rifle close to hand.

Kai, too, always proved a good guard dog. The Siberian husky, with his thick silvery coat, had the look and menacing air of a large timberwolf and few wild animals would care to engage in mortal combat with such a one.

So, in the morning he breakfasted on salt pork, beans and coffee, loaded up his animals and set off on his way. Soon the ascent grew steeper and Scope dismounted to spare Rajah and lead the way. It was no easy nature walk now, but a harsh, hard climb, buffeted by winds that seemed to come at them from all directions and squalls of icy rain. But on they went, up and up, following the hardly discernible trail which zig-zagged up the side of the mountain to the pass.

By late afternoon it looked as if they had made it as the ground flattened out high on the divide. But Scope saw another watershed rising up twenty miles ahead. He stopped to rest awhile, chewing on hardtack, giving the animals a few sugar lumps for energy, then set off again. He wanted to get over the divide and through the icy peaks before a summer blizzard set in.

After that it was plain sailing, as they say. On the far side of this coastal range the streams and watercourses drained down in a northerly direction through numerous lakes and rapids until they fed into the Yukon River. Far off he could see what must be, according to the rough map scrawled out for him by Juneau, the Big Salmon River.

Scope gave a whoop of delight. His route led through country that rolled gently down through grassy valleys all the way to the banks of the Lewes River. 'Whoa, boys,' he yelled, relieving the animals of their burdens. 'Here's a good place to make camp. Dawson City here we come. We should be there in six or seven days.'

At least, that was his hope. But he had an uneasy feeling that he was being followed. He had seen a thin spiral of woodsmoke rising some miles back on the trail and when he reached the heights, looking back he had glimpsed a line of men climbing up through the timber and disappearing from sight. They weren't Indians — there had been numerous massacres in the past in these parts — but he got a prickling at the base of his scalp, an instinct warning him to beware. Maybe they were just prospectors following the same trail. Or maybe they weren't.

Scope carefully oiled the Marlin rifle and levered a slug into the breech. 'Maybe I'd better hang around a bit,' he muttered, 'and see what these bozos want.'

★ ★ ★

'This is preposterous!' Alice Haskell protested. 'Ever since we set out from Skagway we've been robbed blind. We came to this country to get rich, not to go home paupers.'

'Lady, you are entering the British Dominion,' the mountie said. 'The law says you have to pay customs duty on various imported goods. Don't blame me. I'm just carrying out my duty. So you just open those packs and let me take a look.'

'But a dollar a pound on sugar,' Florence Farthing screamed, brandishing a packet in his face. 'That is ridiculous. I'd rather eat it all now than pay that.'

'That's not allowed, madam,' the mountie replied, grabbing hold of the packet. 'If you can't pay it must be forfeited. You're already over the line.'

The packet burst as Florence tried to hang onto it. 'Now look what you've done,' she cried. 'This is iniquitous.'

Alice had chummed up with her on the climb up the Chilcoot Pass. They were both from New York and of the educated class so they had something in common. Both, too, were sick and tired of the endless charges. First there had been a man demanding a toll for the corrugated road — pines laid side by side — he had constructed from

Skagway to Dyea. Then another villain charging them because he claimed to be the one who had cut steps in the ascent of the pass. Plus they had to pay the Indian who wanted five dollars to carry 200 lbs of their gear to the top. At least he had had the decency to only charge two dollars for his squaw's help. And now this!

The log cabin headquarters at the head of the pass was manned by three Mounted Policemen, smartly attired in their little pillbox hats, scarlet jackets, tight britches and shiny riding boots. They carried holstered revolvers on the belts around their waists.

'It's highway robbery,' Florence persisted when informed that a twenty-five per cent tax had to be levied on practically everything the miners were bringing into the country, tools, equipment, guns, clothing, provisions, dogs or horses. 'What are you doing now?'

They had been led into a cabin where their gear was being rummaged through by the officers of the law. A young one, bald but with a dapper moustache, had dug out a cardigan. 'It's a twenty-five per cent payment on woollen goods plus five per cent a pound weight.' He produced a pair of knee-length drawers. 'These too.'

Florence snatched them from him. 'Don't display them to the whole world!'

Another, taller policeman with three gilt stripes on his arm, could not restrain a smile and pointed to a bundle of candles. 'Twenty-eight per cent on them, I'm afraid.'

'You're certainly tightening the cinch,' Alice told him. 'What are you trying to do, stop us all from coming in?'

'I'd like to, but unfortunately that ain't possible, miss.' The sergeant licked his pencil and totted up what she owed the Canadian Government. 'I'd also like proof you have enough funds to support yourself through the winter.'

Alice dipped into her handbag and showed him her roll of notes and silver coins. 'It's fast disappearing,' she sighed.

'It'll go faster soon. You'll find prices in Dawson City are sky high.' The tall mountie signed a receipt to show the taxes had been paid. 'There's one other thing: if you're planning to pan for gold you'll need a Free Miner's Certificate.'

Alice put a hand to her brow and screwed up her eyes. 'How much?'

'Fifteen dollars.'

'Extortion!' Florence howled. 'You're holding us to ransom.'

'Canada for the Canadians,' the bald one retorted. 'If you don't like it, go home. Why should Yanks have all our gold for free?'

'No need for that! He's new out here,' the tall one told Alice. 'We've lost a lot of men, had to bring in new recruits from Winnipeg.'

'How did you lose them?' she asked.

'How do you think, lady? They've deserted. Every man at Fort Cudahy's headed for The Golden Triangle.'

'What?' she cried. 'I heard you were

the most disciplined force in the world.'

He shrugged and counted her money. 'They say a mountie always gets his man. Well, this time it's a case of they've gone to get their gold. *They've* got the fever, too. Move along now, will you?'

'Good Lord,' Alice said, as she dragged her bags outside. 'No wonder Scope went the other way. Now what do we do?'

'You come.' The squat, oval-faced Indian was tugging her sleeve. 'You give.' He held out his palm. 'Five dollar. We go on.' The sixteen-mile climb up through the muddy morass of the pass had been a nightmare. She took five silver dollars from her purse to pay the Indian, and hauled her other heavy bundles on to her shoulders. 'Come on, Florence,' she called. 'The trail surely must get easier from here on.'

The balding Mountie watched them go, his lips smirking beneath his moustache. 'That's what *they* think! These greenhorns, they're unbelievable, ain't they?'

'I don't see what's so funny,' Sergeant Jim MacArthur replied. 'Once winter sets in we could well be stepping over their frozen bodies. Waste of a good woman, if you ask me, particularly the young 'un.'

'Yeah.' His colleague laughed, uproariously. 'That other bossy bitch'd be no great loss. You know, I reckon she must be one of them who talks about their right to vote an' all that. Fair give me the shudders, she did.'

★   ★   ★

Scope Mitchell hid in the shadow of the pines and eased a slug into the breech of the Ballard as he watched and listened, hissing to his dogs to stay quiet. 'Steady, Kai,' he commanded. 'They ain't spotted us.'

From afar it looked like some huge beetle was making its way towards him through the long grass. Closer inspection showed it to be a big birch-bark canoe, its legs those of three men

66

marching along, carrying it over their heads. Frenchie Pete led the way, out on his own, a pack on his back, a rifle held across his chest. In the rear stepped another guard, clothed in fringed buckskins and the red wool-sock hat of a *voyageur*.

They were following the beaten-down track across the mountain meadow that Scope had trod. Pete, in his peaked canvas hat, suddenly looked puzzled as he saw the trail diverted up towards the trees. He raised his rifle, apprehensively, as he sang out to the men to halt. But Scope had circled back and now rode out from the pines behind them. 'Hold it right there, you varmints!' he snapped, ' 'less you all want a bullet in the back.'

Frenchie Pete froze for seconds, then stretched out his arms from his powerful shoulders in his striped woollen shirt, the rifle in his right grip. 'Talk of the devil!' He turned slowly, his swarthy face splitting into a crooked grin. 'We were just wondering how far you were in front, friend.'

'I bet you were. Just throw them rifles aside. Come on, pronto. I got an itchy finger here and I'd just as soon shoot you down for the sneakin' rats y'are. You other three, put that canoe aside and don't try anything, you hear?'

They were a rough-looking bunch and he thought he recognized one of them from the fight a few nights before. 'Hey, you, ain't you brought your chain along today?'

Pete gave a cackle of mirth. 'You got us all wrong, mister. This is a free country, ain't it? We just happen to be going the same way you are.'

The one in the red wool hat pretended to grin, too, but his bared teeth seemed more like a snarl as he tossed his rifle aside. He shouted something in French and spat a gob of baccy.

'Yeah, the same to you, pal.' Scope kneed Rajah closer and Kai emitted a deep-throated growl as he stood poised to attack beside him. 'OK, you all move back in line where I can keep an eye on you.'

'Keep that dog away from me, mister.' The squat, frog-like desperado who had swung the chain, pointed a finger at Kai. 'Or I'll stick my knife in his throat, I swear.'

'You won't be sticking it in nobody right now,' Scope replied coolly levelling the Ballard in his direction. 'You pull it out nice 'n slow and stick it in the turf.' The man hesitated, nervously glancing at the others, but did as he was bid. 'That's better,' Scope said. 'Now how about that one in your boot?'

When the thug had safely surrendered that, too, Scope ordered, 'Now, the rest of you, I want any weapons you're carrying. Toss 'em down on the grass.'

'You can't do this,' Pete shouted. 'You got no right.'

'Right? What right did you give me the other night? You chose the wrong fella, as it happens. But what rights did you give all them other poor devils you've robbed?'

As the five men reluctantly removed

heavy revolvers from their belts, knives from sheaths, and, at Scope's insistence, blackjacks and brass knuckles from coat pockets, he slid the Ballard back into the saddle holster and whipped out his Iver Johnson nickel-plated revolver. The .38 calibre could stop any man in his tracks at close distance and, of course, did not require cocking.

'I got six trusty friends in here,' he gritted out stepping down. 'Enough to take each one of you out with the help of my dogs. I'd just as soon kill you all and leave your carcasses for the ravens.'

Pete cursed in French and shrugged his shoulders with Gallic expression, 'Hey, meester, we don' wanna hurt you. We just wanna get to the goldfields. Why you do this?'

Scope gripped the solid rubber butt plates of the revolver. The triple action had a unique safety feature, with the hammer resting against the steel frame rather than the firing pin. Its disadvantage, in one way, was that it required a long, firm pull, enabling a man to choose his targets more accurately, which made it no fast shooter. However, they weren't to know that.

'I'm doing this,' he drawled, as he kept them covered, 'because I don't want any of you smelly skunks creepin' up on me in my camp.' He bent down and picked up the weapons one by one, hurling them away as hard as he could into the rocks and trees. The revolvers he emptied of their slugs into his own pockets and threw them away, too. The two rifles he smashed against the rocks and tossed aside.

'*Sacre bleu!*' Pete wailed. 'You can't do that. That's a fifty-dollar rifle.'

'It was,' Scope replied, drily as he brandished one of their vicious hunting knives in his left hand. 'Come here, you oily louse.'

'What you wan'?' Pete demurred, looking alarmed.

'Step up here. Or would you rather have a bullet in your chest?'

When Frenchie Pete stepped forward

Scope scooped the knife up through the belt of his pants and quickly sawed it through. 'You wear braces, too, huh?' He nicked them through, too. 'Now take your boots off and drop your pants.'

'What?' Pete cursed loudly in French but obeyed. 'You rotten bastard.'

Scope grinned and hurled the boots, too, into the woods. Then, one by one, he gave the others the same treatment. When the one who had wielded the chain refused, he slammed the revolver across his ugly jaw and he spat blood and complied.

'So long, boys.' Scope swung back up on to the gelding. 'That should slow you up a bit.' He went charging away on Rajah, followed by the dogs, and turned to call back, 'Have a nice day.'

He slid the Iver Johnson back in the holster on his belt and muttered, 'Maybe I shoulda smashed a hole in that canoe, but, hell, I'm feelin' generous today.'

5

Alice Haskell was amazed to see that a city of tents had sprung up in the wilderness when, led by her Chilcoot 'packjack', she tottered along the shore of the thirty-mile-long Lake Bennett. There were canvas hotels, restaurants and even clapboard saloons and dance halls where wanton women plied their trade.

'At least we should be able to rest our feet awhile,' Florence cried, as she hugged her bundles under her arms and trudged along behind her own Indian bearer. 'You can put my pack down here,' she ordered, as they reached the hive of activity. 'There's nothing I'd like better than a nice cup of tea.'

It had been a long trek indeed, coming down from the divide through the rugged terrain, past Long Lake and Deep Lake, their guides urging them on.

'What do we do now?' Alice wondered, as they paid an exorbitant five dollars for a pot of pine needle tea, sitting on the ground in the shade of the tent café.

'You build yourself a boat like everybody else and head on down the rapids,' the owner remarked, as he pocketed the cash.

'But, how do we do that?' Florence protested. 'We haven't brought saws, or nails, or even rope.' The nostrils of her bony, aristocratic nose twitched with disdain as she flicked the flies from a syrup flapjack provided for her consumption at further expense.

'Perhaps we could buy one?' Alice suggested, but it was a faint hope for they were but two of 30,000 folk who that summer were trying to follow the 575-mile trail from the beaches, across the mountains and along the lakes and rivers to the gold fields. Already 2,000 or so had given up and turned back.

'There's a young fella along the beach hiring himself out as a pilot,' the waiter told them. 'He might have room on his raft for yuh, if you can afford him.'

'Come on,' Alice said. 'Let's go find him. We're wasting time here.'

The weather was sultry, the temperature in the nineties, and Alice felt exhausted as they dragged their bundles along the beach, but she only knew they had to keep going with all haste.

He was certainly a lusty-looking character, stripped to the waist, barrel-chested, with sturdy arms as he loaded a big raft he had built. He cheerfully introduced himself as Jack London, an educated man and would-be writer. His prices were educational, too. He wanted fifty dollars each to take them through.

Alice dug deep into her bag and produced the necessary, and he tucked it into a leather wallet on his hip already as fat as a melon, stuffed with silver, gold and notes. There were six other passengers on the raft, with their 1,000 lb loads of gear, and it appeared to be low in the water and listing danger-ously. But Jack battened down the ladies' baggage and poled them away into deep water.

'We're on our way,' Alice cried, with a sunny smile, as the sound of sawing and hammering at various makeshift boats receded with the shoreline. There were some amazing floating contraptions, wherries with blanket sails, others with rudders and cabins. London's was a twenty-foot long raft, with a six-foot beam and pointed prow. He hung on to a big steering sweep as they drifted out on to the current and grinned at the girls. 'It might be best for you ladies to rope yourself to that rail 'fore we reach the rapids,' he shouted, 'but that won't be for a while.'

Indeed, progress was slow at first, Jack abandoning the sweep to pole them through driftwood and sandbars as the riverway coiled into Tagish Lake, past an Indian village and Caribou Crossing. The red-stained mountains with their crowns of ice and the blue glaciers began to fall away into the distance.

Alice had rigged a netting veil over her large hat, tucked into her costume at the neck, for some protection against the clouds of mosquitoes and gnats, while Florence swung a wet towel at them. For twenty hours the sun burned down relentlessly until a brief twilight settled around them.

Beyond Tagish they entered a twenty-mile bowl of mud named Lake Marsh, with dreary banks of silt on either side. All were more than glad to see the end of it as the raft slid silently out into the swift current of Fifty Mile River.

'Here's where I have to keep a sharp look-out, the snags and rocks and twists and turns have wrecked many a raftsman,' Jack shouted. And he wasn't kidding. After thirty miles of calm rafting suddenly the river narrowed between high stone walls and shot from sight. 'Hang on, folks.'

'Oh, my God!' Alice muttered, as an ominous murmur became a deafening roar. They were sucked into a narrow gate, in to the basalt walls of Miles Canyon and the raft was pulled away in a side-sweeping roll surely towards imminent destruction.

Jack's face set grimly as he hung on to the sweep in a mammoth effort to keep the tossing, spinning raft away from an evil-looking whirlpool known as The Squaw. The thunder of water reverberating against the steep sides of the gorge was deafening, and all Alice could do was hang on for precious life as she heard Florence's shrill screams of fear.

But that was only the start of it. For two more miles the river raced on until it narrowed again and plunged into a twenty-foot sluice that was even more abrupt and dangerous than Miles. They hit white water, waves tossing and bucking them about in the wildest confusion, some fifteen feet high washing over them, trying to drag them from their fragile craft. On they were swept, buffeted like a cork, on into

White Horse Rapids and more turmoil.

Suddenly it was over as the churning water bubbled more slowly and fed them into the calmer waters of Lake Lebarge. Jack rested his elbows on the sweep and lit a cigarette. 'Well, how'd ya like the ride? We shot in an' out of there faster than I could spit. Y'all look like drowned rats! Ye can dry out at McCauley's roadhouse.'

Lo and behold a ramshackle log cabin came into sight and Jack poled them into the bank. He laughed, exuberantly, as he helped the women ashore. No doubt his bravado was tinged with relief that he had got through once more for 200 boat people had been drowned, sucked into the Squaw that summer.

McCauley was in a merry mood because a raft carrying twenty barrels of whiskey had capsized coming through the day before and they had all washed up on his beach. The burly Irishman greeted Jack with open arms and pressed a clay mug of hooch into his hands. 'Just the boyo I was wanting to meet to have a good jaw with.'

The women and the others were told to help themselves to boiled slices of salmon caught that morning, but first they retired behind a suspended blanket and dragged off their sodden clothes to dry out in the sunshine. Alice had taken a liking to Jack and when, eventually, she had pulled a comb through her hair, eaten, and made herself respectable she went to look for him. But it seemed that London was a slave to whiskey. His words were slurred, his eyes glazed, and he was babbling incoherently to McCauley. He rose to greet her but could hardly stay on his feet as he swayed. 'I was just saying all that fussy, genteel literature you probably like, lady, is as dead as the dodo,' he shouted at her. 'We're nearing the turn of the century and from now on we write about reality. I'm the voice of the future.'

Alice excused herself and joined Florence. They got as much sleep as they could on bare planks in a corner of the cabin and several hours later found Jack still drinking. 'Take the raft,' he said, waving his hand. 'It's easy now. There's only Five Finger Rapids after you join the Big Salmon. But they're a piece of cake. Then you'll soon be at Fort Selkirk and swept on your way to Dawson City. You can't miss it.'

'What are you going to do?' Alice asked, with some alarm.

'I'm gonna have me a good time. Then I'm going back to build another raft and pick up some more paying passengers. This money's too good to miss.' Jack grinned drunkenly at her as he offered his hand. 'Nice to have met you, Alice. Good luck.'

'Yes,' she said, 'I think I'm going to need it.'

★ ★ ★

Dawson City, at the confluence of the Yukon and the Klondike rivers, was a bustling centre of activity, scows lined up two or three deep along the water-front when Scope poled his raft in to join them. He had constructed a horse-box of poles in centre to hold Rajah. But by going the land route he had missed the rapids so it had been a calm passage.

'Let's go take a look at the town,' he called to the dogs after he had got the horse on to dry land.

The summer before there had been a transient population of some 300 trappers and sourdoughs. Now there were 3,000 thronging Front Street where company stores, log cabins, saloons, hotels, a post office and a Mounted Police post had been built, the Union Jack flapping from a mast. Behind these stretched a shanty town of shacks and tents.

'Teeth pulled — two dollars', proclaimed a sign. Many of the cheechakos, as the fortune hunters were generally termed, had decided there was more money to be made plying their own professions. Lawyers, real estate agents, goldsmiths, barbers, timber merchants, undertakers, fortune-tellers, purveyors of medicines and instant cure-alls thrived.

Prices were sky-high, as Scope discovered when, rifle under his arm, he stepped into Tim Rickards' house of pleasure. It was a bedlam of long-haired, buckskin-clad pioneers, gamblers, city dudes, riff-raff and screaming girls. Whiskey was fifty cents a shot and when Scope asked the 'keep for a cigar it set him back $1.50.

'Ouch!' he said, 'I'd better take it easy.'

Prospectors were clamouring to pay with pouches of gold dust, getting it weighed at the bar, exchanging it for chips for the 'dancing girls' or to get into one of the innumerable games of chance, faro, *rouge et noir*, or roulette. A 'shotgun' sat on a raised chair and kept a watchful eye out for trouble.

'Jeez!' Scope gave a whistle of awe under his breath as he took a sip of the hooch that tasted distinctly watered-down, and suddenly realized that men were chancing $1,000 throws on the roll of a dice.

'Does this go on all the time?' he asked an older man.

The top-hatted part-Indian with gold teeth, grinned at him. 'Day and night, mister. Never ceases. This ain't nuthin'. Thar's a five thousand dollar pot in the poker game over in the corner. The sky's the limit, boy. Why? You wanna jine in?'

'Not jest yet. Maybe when I come back.'

'Hech! Ye'll be lucky. That's millionaires' corner over there.'

'Yeah, well, I've got as good a chance of comin' back rich as anybody, ain't I?'

'You keep thinkin' that,' the long-haired half-breed replied. 'There's thousands come back from the creeks with barely enough dust to keep body and soul alive.'

Scope decided to invest in a bottle for five dollars and invited Skookum Jim, as he was called, to share it. He had been in Yukon territory all his life, had wed into an Indian tribe, so his head surely contained much vital information.

He had a hard job hearing what Jim had to say as he pumped him, what with drunken miners fighting to dance with the girls and a black fellow in a loud suit and bow tie jangling a piano on a podium and singing, 'There'll be a hot time in the old town tonight.' He sure enough wasn't kidding!

But when he got back to his horse and dogs he had plenty to chew on. 'Come on, boys,' he shouted as he swung aboard Rajah. 'Let's be going. We ain't no time to lose if we're gonna make our fortune.'

★　★　★

Frenchie Pete and his pals had wasted hours searching for their revolvers, boots, knives and knuckles in the thick underbrush where they had been hurled by the young American. They cursed, vociferously, as they regarded their cut-apart belts and braces and searched for bits of string to secure their trousers before picking up their canoe again. 'I cannot wait to kill him,' one of them, nicknamed Couteau, hissed. 'What pleasure it will be to pull my knife slowly across his throat.'

'You will have to wait,' Frenchie Pete told them. 'My orders are to keep a watch on him. We think he is on to something. He was seen talking to Juneau. We watch, we wait, then we kill him.'

That would be a sweeter revenge. Let him break his back digging for his gold then, when he came in, take it from him. They would take that girl, too, who had held the rifle on them. 'Don't worry,' he growled. 'We'll have our fun.'

★ ★ ★

Scope rode for sixteen miles along the bank of the narrow, turbulent Klondike, turning into Hunker Creek, up towards the thickly forested mountains and the peak known as The Dome. Yes, he was

86

on the right track. His mine wouldn't be far away now, up a subsidiary stream known as Gold Bottom. All along the creeks men were bent double, digging and sluicing, or simply panning for gold. They waved him impatiently on his way when he showed them his claim form.

'This is it, number one two three,' he muttered when he saw the staves marked with the claim number hammered in the ground for 500 paces along the creek. 'That's funny, what's this fella up to?'

A scruffy man, with a long, pointed beard, had emerged from a deep hole, a shovel in his hands and scowled at him. 'You want something, son?'

'Yeah, this is my claim.' He got from his horse and waved the creased form at him. 'I bought it from Joe Juneau for two hundred dollars, fair and square.'

The gnarled gnome from the bowels of the earth took a squint at it. 'Rubbish. This is out of date. It ain't worth a cent, sonny.'

'Whatja mean?' Scope demanded.

'Ain't you heard, boy? The gov'ment's brought in a new rule. Any claim abandoned for more than seventy-two hours is deemed fair game for anybody who comes along. That happened to be me. I been workin' here all summer.'

It was like a hammer blow to Scope's hopes. Two hundred precious dollars up the creek, as they say. 'Are you sure?'

'Sure I'm sure. You better clear off and ask the mounties if you don't believe me. Don't come here toting them guns tryin' to jump my claim, pal.'

'I ain't tryin' to jump you, mister. I guess I'll have to look someplace else. Any ideas where I can try?'

'You better go back to the Bonanza or Eldorado. That's where the big strikes are. But ye'll need more than two hundred dollars for a claim along there.'

Scope gave a grimace of displeasure and turned back to Rajah. One foot in the stirrup he paused. 'Say,' he called, 'just outa interest, you got anything much outa here?'

'Not a lot.' The miner eyed him, craftily, then grinned broadly. 'About twenty thousand dollars last count.'

'You don't say. Is that all? Hardly worth bothering with.' Scope turned the horse and rode back down the marshy creek, looking for a place to camp. 'So Joe was right,' he muttered. 'Dig deep, he said. I guess he didn't know about this new law. Waal, we'll have to give him the benefit of the doubt, eh, boys?'

When he spotted a mallard sitting on its nest in the reeds twenty paces away he slipped his lariat from the saddle horn and sent it spinning across to neatly loop over its head. He jerked it tight and hauled the struggling, squawking creature to him. He caught it and with an expert twist broke its neck. 'Sorry, ducky, but I'm kinda hungry. Life ain't fair, is it?'

Two hours later he was hunkered down beneath an overhang of rock before the glowing embers of his fire feasting on tender slices of duck breast and an omelette made from the rich eggs, tossing bits of fatty skin, the legs and wings to the dogs.

'Don't worry, boys,' he said, lying back against his saddle. 'There's plenty of gold in these hyar hills an' I'm gonna git my share of it.'

6

Alice, Florence and their party had made good time on Jack London's solid raft. Once past Fort Selkirk they entered the Yukon's full stream, travelling for 100 miles through splendid parapets of stone and on through a myriad of evergreen islands, covering sixty or seventy miles a day. When they found a place to beach amid all the craft drawn up at Dawson, their male companions hurried off with their heavy gear.

'Wait a minute!' Florence cried. 'The raft's made of good solid logs. They would make the start of a cabin. Can you help me carry them up to the town, Alice?'

The girl, too, was impatient to be off to look for gold. 'What do you want a cabin here for? Aren't you coming with me?'

'Not likely. This town is where the money's to be made. What do we know about digging for gold?'

'Well, I'll give you a hand, but then I've got to go.' She watched the older woman, who had pulled a carving knife from her sack and was already sawing at the ropes of the raft. 'Hadn't you better find yourself a site first?'

'Good thinking.' However, to her astonishment Florence found that all the prime sites on Front Street had been snapped up. There was only one lot for sale and that was going for an astronomical $500. 'Good gracious!' Florence fanned at the flies, her bony face a frown of thought. 'I'll take it.' She dug in her bag and produced the cash in greenbacks. 'Good,' she smiled. 'I'm in business now.'

When they had hauled the pine stakes up to the vacant lot Florence had another shock. Labourers back home would have cost less than four dollars a day. Here no man was willing to work for less than fifteen. 'It looks like I'll have to build it myself,' she said. 'Don't you worry, Alice. I'm going into buying and selling gold.'

Another shock was having to shell out fifteen dollars for a bowl of canned oyster stew in the nearby arcade restaurant, but they were getting used to boom-town prices. 'To tell the truth I'm happy about it,' Florence remarked. 'I'm making a note of the most expensive items in demand. I'll order a shipment to be sent in. For instance, some of these young hussies around town would pay the earth to be seen in a new ostrich boa.'

Three shallow-draught paddle steamers had by now made the long, circuitous journey up the Yukon from St Michael in the far north and were anchored off the town. 'You see!' Florence waved airily. 'Anything is possible.'

'At least you're close to the mountie post,' Alice remarked, as they stepped on to the ankle-deep mud of the street. The post consisted of a number of log houses arranged around three sides of a central square. 'In case of trouble,' she added. But then her heart seemed to sink into her boots for who should step out of Rickards' saloon but Frenchie Pete.

'Waal, whadda ya know?' His dark, scarred face split into an evil grin as he beckoned to four unsavoury-looking, drunken men spilling from the hell hole. 'Li'l Annie Oakley, but she ain't got her gun today.'

The men guffawed, sneering in French *patois* at the two women, lurching unsteadily towards them. One in a red sock hat poked a finger at Alice's chest. 'Is thees the cookie we gonna have?'

'That's her.' A greasy squat man, who the girl remembered wielding a chain in the alleyway, also prodded a forefinger at her. 'That's the bitch who tried to shoot us.'

'How dare you, you insolent oaf,' Florence screeched, hitting the *voyageur* a sharp blow with her parasol.

'How dare you insult an American lady.'

For reply, the Frenchman snatched the parasol and broke it across his knee, pushing Florence so hard she fell back and collapsed in the mud. 'You keep out of this, horseface.'

'*Oui*, you come with us, *ma'mselle*.' Pete grabbed hold of Alice's arm and began to drag her away. 'We got business with you.'

The girl struggled to escape, but the men had hard hold of her. Suddenly a gunshot cracked out and they all froze for seconds, then turned as an authoritative voice shouted, 'What in hell's going on?'

The tall redcoat Jim MacArthur was standing ten feet away, an upraised revolver held in his hand. 'Take your hands off that girl.'

'*Merde!*' The squat Frenchman pulled back his ragged coat, his fingers moving towards a heavy Colt stuffed in his new belt, letting out a string of curses as he stared at the mountie.

'Don't be a fool!' Pete hissed, holding him back, and he gave his broken-toothed, ingratiating smile. 'What's wrong, officer? You are just the man we want to see. We are making a citizen's arrest. Thees harlot try to keel us in Skagway. She fire on us with rifle — '

'That I find hard to believe,' the officer replied. 'Nor do I think it wise to try to blemish her reputation.'

'It's true,' Alice cried, pulling away from them. 'I fired on them, but only because they were beating up a friend of mine.'

'That I am more inclined to believe.'

'Ah, *oui*, you would take the side of the pretty girl,' Frenchie Pete sneered. 'I want to make charge against her.'

'Ridiculous!' Florence had regained her feet. 'It's these men, if you can call them men, who you must charge. Did you see how the cowardly scum attacked me? Is this how Canadians behave?'

A smile flickered on the mountie's lips. 'No, madam, not all of us. All right, you men, put up your hands. I'm taking you in. You two ladies had better come, too. We'll sort this out at the post.'

After much drunken arguing the five Frenchmen were thrown into a cell. 'You'll be up in court in the morning,' the mountie told them.

'What will happen to them?' Alice asked, glancing up at the tall Britisher as he escorted her and Florence from the post.

'That depends on your evidence, but they'll probably be fined and put to chopping logs for the woodpile for a couple of days. There's not a lot I can charge them with.'

'At least that'll give me a chance to get out of the way. I'm afraid they still intend to carry out their threats.'

'They'll get a good strong warning. I wouldn't worry too much. I think this was drunken bravado.'

Alice wasn't so sure, but tried to put on a brave face. 'Is there anywhere I can buy a horse to transport my stuff and get well away?'

'There's only a dozen horses around

this place, not much hope of that.' Jim grinned at her in a fatherly way. 'So, you're going prospectin'?'

'Yes, all by myself. Florence is staying here.'

'Without any protection, or knowledge of the country? I don't advise it.'

'I've got to go. I must. I have family debts I've got to clear. I've come all this way. I must try.'

'I did hear a fellow say he had had enough and was going home. Yes, he had a mule he'll be selling, if it hasn't already gone.'

'Really?' Alice touched his scarlet-coated arm. and smiled up at him. 'Would you . . . could you possibly help me find him?'

Sergeant MacArthur clicked the heels of his shiny boots and saluted. 'It would be a pleasure, my dear.'

* * *

The Golden Triangle was bounded by the Yukon and Klondike rivers and a ridge of mountains dominated by The Dome forming the third side. The whole country was swampy pasture for moose and caribou before the herds moved out and men moved in to devastate the banks of every little creek and inlet with their digging. The most populous was Bonanza, running on into Eldorado which, by the time Scope arrived, was staked from end to end.

The Bonanza trail was wet all summer long, slippery with mud. He had to continually make his way around dumps and holes, cabins, sluices and dams. Eventually he reached Grand Forks where Belinda Mulrooney ran a two-storey hotel of sorts. The bar-room was packed, a noisy, spirited meeting of miners in progress.

Scope bought a beer and discovered that the indignation was caused by the government commissioner's new law that each man should be limited to only one claim. Most miners had several and would 'shut up shop' as they dashed off to a new rush to check it out.

'Everybody hates the gold commissioner's guts, but he's got the law behind him and what he says goes,' the burly Belinda yelled, as she conducted an auction of claims. 'So come on, let's hear which ones you're giving up.'

'Looks like I've arrived just in time,' Scope muttered. It was standing room only and new prospectors like himself were vying to make bids. Most of the surplus claims were snapped up for $300 or $450, which created a problem because Scope was now all but broke.

There was a chorus of laughter when an old-timer, a Swede called Charlie Anderson offered his claim on Sixty Mile River. 'I wouldn't give you a shovel for it,' a cheechako yelled.

Charlie, who was already six sheets to the wind, held out for a shovel and a mule, but, like many bedraggled sourdoughs had a pouch of dust in his pocket. His lifetime's earnings, it weighed out at $750. 'Anybody got a claim to offer on Eldorado?' he shouted, waving his pouch. He parted with it for the untried claim, twenty-nine. When he sobered up he demanded his money back, but in vain.

However, against that sort of competition Scope had no chance.

'How about them claims up on Skookum Creek?' Belinda yelled, and again everybody cackled their derision. 'It ain't no good hangin' on to 'em if you're gonna try someplace else.'

When several went for $150 or so, Scope offered $30 for the last up, plus a big bag of beans and his precious tobacco, equivalent in those parts to about $100. 'Sold to the handsome young gent in the Stetson,' Belinda cried, with a cheeky grin his way. 'Call in an' see me when you're in the money, cowboy.'

★ ★ ★

When he left Bonanza and headed up Eldorado the trail became drier as it rose towards the ridge of hills. Scope rode for fifteen miles, dragging his gear on the travois and followed by the dogs. Klondike gold was found in two places, at first in the creek beds where a panhandler might get twelve dollars in glittery bits out of two shovelfuls of gravel sifted at the creek side. Then, months later on the hilltops, which were called benches.

When he reached a sign pointing up the narrow Skookum Creek Scope was surprised to learn that it had been named after the man he had met in Tim Rickards' saloon. And there he was, half way up, in his stovepipe hat, sitting on a pile of rocks enjoying a rest and a tin mug of coffee.

'What do you want up here?' he asked.

Scope waved his claim form at him. 'Number sixty-nine.' He grinned at Jim. 'Looks like we're gonna be neighbours.'

Skookum examined the certificate. 'You're right at the top. Ain't nuthin' much been found up there yet.' He poured a cup of black coffee from his enamel pot and passed it across. 'I figure you'll need to dig a shaft deep into the hillside. That's what puts most men off.'

Miners had scraped up most of the gold from the benches, he explained, rich accumulations barely covered. 'They think the surface dirt is the exposed bedrock. After they get it up they rush off to look for more riches under the moss and abandon their claims. Most just ain't got no dedication.'

'So you reckon it's gonna take me a while 'fore I find anything?'

'Just keep digging, boy. Sooner or later you'll hit a seam.' Jim's solid gold teeth glinted as he jawed. 'The only trouble is it's mid-August already. In another four or five weeks the snows will start. There ain't many git much done once winter sets in. You have to hang on an' wait 'til spring. You got enough supplies to see you through?'

'Waal, I dunno, I had to pay for this claim with my beans and baccy.' Scope tossed away the dregs from the tin mug and patted his rifle. 'I'm planning to git me a moose or two, or maybe a bear. But if what you say is right I'd better be making a start up there.'

As he set off up the steep trail Skookum Jim called out, 'You'll be needin' a sled for them dogs. I might be able to help you there.'

When he got to the top of the hill Scope was faced by a solid wall of rock which rose to a peak. The land at the foot of it was clearly marked with pegs for 500 ft. as his claim. There was the remains of a ramshackle cabin and not much else except for piles of dirt where the top-surface had been scooped off.

Scope tipped his Stetson over his forehead and scratched the back of his head. 'It sure don't look very promising, does it, boys?' He was glad to note that there were some stands of timber along the ridge. 'First thing to do is repair this cabin and git in a supply of firewood.'

The sound of his axe chopping as he felled trees filled the air for the next three days. He had decided to pull down most of the rotten old cabin and start from scratch. He built it against the wall of the cliff on a platform of rocks and logs, first raising the walls, with a side door away from the wind, then finding some solid beams from a fallen cypress and, with the help of Rajah, dragging them back to try to construct a sloping roof that would shed snow. He rigged up a kind of larch-pole derrick and used horse power to hoist up the cypress beams and set them in place. It was a dangerous operation. If a beam had slipped it could have crushed him, but by sheer strength and willpower he finally had it looking shipshape.

Luckily, the last occupant of the claim had abandoned his tin stove. Scope rigged it up in the middle of the room so the tin chimney poked out from the side of a wall and hopefully wouldn't get blocked by snow.

'There we are,' he said, finally lighting up and watching the glow as he put his coffee pot on to boil. 'Home sweet home.'

He spent another three days hauling up pine branches, moss and buckets of earth to make the roof waterproof, and caulked any holes in the walls with moss and mud. But precious time was running out and it didn't look like he was going to get much mining done before the dark days set in.

'This looks as good as any place to start,' he muttered, examining a declivity in the cliff at a safe distance away from the cabin. 'But it's gonna take a hell of a lot of digging.'

He had, however, bought a half-dozen sticks of dynamite in Dawson, at considerable cost, which he would be able to use sparingly once he had made an entry into the rock. He stripped off his shirt and wielded his pick-axe to make the first strike. The summer sun blazed down on his back, and even though there was a cooling mountain breeze, sweat was soon pouring from his body. After three hours he paused to take a short rest.

'Jeez,' he whispered. 'I ain't made much of an impression yet.'

He picked up his goatskin water bottle, took a swig and wiped sweat from his armpits. The dogs were lazing around watching him. Suddenly Kai gave a warning growl, which set them all off howling.

'Quiet!' he yelled and glanced around to see where he had left his rifle. He peered down through the rocks of the creek and saw a grey-clothed figure approaching, leading a mule laden with tarpaulin-covered sacks. A large hat, a tight-waisted costume and long skirt: a woman, in fact. 'Waal, whadda ya know?' Scope drawled.

As she drew close, Alice Haskell peered up at him and seemed equally surprised. 'Mr Mitchell! What are you doing here?'

'What does it look like?' He brandished the pick. 'I've bought this claim.'

'Really?' She hauled the mule up higher beside her. 'This bothersome

107

creature. I do believe he's demented. He always wants to go in the opposite direction to the one I want to take. Still, I suppose I'm lucky to have got him.'

As the mule started loudly braying in protest, Scope grinned and drawled, 'Them critters sure can be stubborn as hell.'

Alice took off her hat and wiped a hand across her brow. 'Are there any more claims up here for sale?'

'Nope. This here's a dead end. Looks like I got the last one. There's another creek runs parallel to this further up the Eldorado. Maybe you should try that.'

A look of exasperation crossed the girl's face as she gave a gasp of weariness. 'I've tried everywhere but nobody seems willing to sell except at an absurdly high price.' She studied his muscular physique and gave a slight smile. 'You look busy. I'd better not keep you.'

She started to turn away, but Scope called out, 'Hang on a minute. I was just thinkin' of havin' a cup of cawfee. You want one? Tie up that critter and come on along. Don't worry about the dogs. Hey, look, Kai remembers you.'

The husky was wagging his rudder furiously as Alice bent to fondle him. 'Yes, you remember me from the boat, don't you, boy?'

When they reached the cabin he invited her in and she looked around at the bed of pine boughs on a raised platform, and his saddle chair. 'Well, you seem to have made yourself comfortable.'

'Take a seat,' he said, stoking the stove and crushing coffee beans with his revolver butt. 'I ain't got properly organized yet, but I'm hoping to survive the blizzards.'

Alice perched on the saddle and watched him with a touch of wistful envy. 'I guess I'd better find somewhere soon and dig in for the winter too.'

Scope glanced at her. 'Yeah, I reckon you had. You could always cross the divide. They reckon there's gold to be found on Sulphur Creek off the Indian River.

'Yes, I suppose I could,' she said, but that sounded a daunting prospect to the girl. 'I'd hate to have to go back to Dawson. Have you found anything yet?'

'Nope, but I'm hopeful. This creek was carved out by some ancient glacier aeons ago and that's where the gold lies, in the creeks. I'm making a wild bet there's a vein goes on up under this peak. Of course I could be wrong an' all my work will have been in vain. Plenty of men have come out with nuthin. What I would do then, I dunno, maybe start a dog-sleddin' business. But I'm gonna give this rock a try first.'

'Good for you.' The girl sipped at the scalding brew. 'A very spartan existence. I hope it pays off for you. Of course, Florence did offer to take me into partnership so maybe I'll take her up on that.'

'Waal, Alice, to be frank there ain't many can face this sort of work or the rigours of a winter out on their own. If I might say, you oughta strongly think about going back to Dawson 'fore it's too late.'

'Yes, I suppose I must.' Alice Haskell gave a deep sigh and got to her feet. 'But first I'll take a look at that next creek you mentioned.'

'Can I offer you a bite to eat 'fore you go?' Scope asked. 'You gotta keep up your strength.'

'No, I'd better be on my way,' Alice said, as they stepped out into the sunshine. 'It's very kind of you.'

He watched her return to the 'bothersome' mule, and called out, 'Hey, how about you work with me?'

Alice turned to him. 'How do you mean?'

'Well, I've already got to go half shares with my backer. But, seeing as I'm likely to be doing most of the hard work I could cut you in for a third of what I take. You could make yourself useful around the place.'

A wary smile spread over Alice's face. 'By useful that presumably includes

111

sharing your bed with you?'

'Waal,' he drawled, his smile widening, 'that might be nice, too. Give us somethun' to do winter evenings.'

'Forget it,' she said. 'I've told you before I'm not planning on going home pregnant.'

He watched her for a while as she tried to turn the mule in the narrow trail. 'You know,' he called, 'you ain't gonna make it out here on your own. They'll be pickin' up your frozen body come springtime.'

'I don't care,' she replied, testily. 'I can't agree to your terms. I'll survive.'

'All right,' he shouted. 'You're as stubborn as that durn mule. I guess I'll be working so hard stayin' celibate won't bother me.'

'A third of your share?'

'That's the agreement.'

She smiled brightly and climbed up to him, sticking out her hand to shake his. 'Nice to meet you, partner. I only hope I can trust you to keep your side of the bargain.'

He grunted, dolefully. 'I only hope I can trust myself.' He had an urge right then to pull the girl into him and put his arms around her. But he released her hand. 'We'd better git busy,' he said.

7

Frenchie Pete peered down through the pines at the cabin below the jutting rock peak. The young American was using his horse to drag a raft of poles loaded with dirt and stones out of the hole he had dug at the base of the cliff. The girl in her dust-bedraggled costume was standing nearby with a shovel in her hands.

'So that is where the bitch has got to, is it?' he muttered. 'Moved in with that punk? Having fun with her, is he? Soon he won't be the only one, eh, Couteau?'

His squat companion had earned the name Knife for his murderous ability with a blade and, as he knelt beside Frenchie, he laughed, gutturally, and growled, 'No, he sure won't.'

The horse had dragged the raft to the rain-swollen stream and the girl was helping Mitchell shovel the muck into a rocker. They worked for a while, bent over, sluicing the sludge away and plodding with the horse back up to their hole.

'Have they found anything?' Couteau asked.

'It don't look like it.' Pete hugged a Mauser rifle into his shoulder, and squinted along the sights. He had stolen it, with other valuables, from an ex-Indian Army Englisher they had encountered along the trail and left his bleeding body in the swamp. Frenchie had the pinhead sight aligned in the v-notch aimed at the American's back and lovingly took first pressure on the trigger. 'Maybe I'd better wait and see what the boss says,' he breathed out. 'Come on, let's get back to the others.'

Down by his mine Scope heard Kai growl and glanced around at the dark woods. He had an uneasy feeling he was being watched, but shrugged it off. Maybe it was just a wolverine or bear on the prowl. He was too busy to go investigate. All along the thirty miles of creeks men were working twenty hours a day, frantic to find what they could before the winter set in and the ground froze solid as rock. And Scope was no exception. Alice was proving an eager worker, too, helping to clear away the scree, gradually getting the hang of chopping logs for their woodpile, and making herself handy lighting the stove, baking their bread, preparing their meal in readiness for when he returned to the cabin. He would be exhausted and hungry and interested only in getting a few hours' sleep during the brief twilight.

A woman's touch was welcome, too, for she swept and tidied the cabin and had rigged up a kind of table on four log legs for them to squat down, Japanese style, to eat their meals. She washed his spare shirt and sewed his torn clothes and, all in all, was pleasant to have around.

Alice had paused for a rest to look out at the creeks scrolling through the gulches in patterns of their own. They

116

gave no indication of where the paystreaks might be. The miners had to just dig and hope for the best.

The sun was already beginning to sink lower in the sky, its golden rays filtering through patches of aspens shimmering bright yellow amid the evergreens. 'It is such a vast and awesome land, quite beautiful in its way,' she remarked. 'I wish I had brought my painting set.'

Scope couldn't help but smile at her bright eyes and pert, intelligent face. 'We ain't got time for looking at the scenery, gal. We got work to do.'

As for their sleeping arrangements, he had rigged up a pine-bough bed for her, but, on her instruction, placed it on the far side of the stove from him. She would undress, modestly, beneath a blanket and, in spite of his blistered hands and weariness from the strenu-ous work, her rustling clothes in the confined space had become a kind of aphrodisiac to his carnal senses. Try as he might to ignore her it was not easy.

In this warm weather Alice would find a secluded spot further up the creek to wash her body, but he wondered what she would do when cold weather confined them to the cabin, if she were still with him then.

For the moment he was intent on boring into his mine and had already used three sticks of dynamite to open it up. It took hours to pick-axe a hole in the rock deep enough to insert a stick, then light the fuse and retire hurriedly to a safe spot. A muffled explosion and dust and rocks would billow out. Then they would have to start clearing it out.

It was a risky business; ever present the danger of the small mine caving in on him, but he tried to prop the roof firm with pine poles and worked on . . . and on . . . and on . . . with no sign of any paydirt.

Scope wiped the dust from his sweat-streaked face and muttered, 'Maybe there ain't nuthin' here. Maybe I oughta try another spot.'

'Don't give up yet,' Alice encouraged.

'Surely we must find something soon.' She had taken the advice of the wife of Horace Berry in the Seattle news-sheet and had started poking around underneath rocks in the creek and had found small nuggets half the size of her little fingernail. Not many, but enough to trade for coffee down at Belinda's hotel. 'There must be more gold here.'

'Sure, but where? I ain't seen a sign of it. This is like playing blind man's buff.'

★　★　★

They were well into September and Alice was washing their tin plates when she heard a wild shout from Scope.

'*Eureka!*' He was dancing about at the mouth of the cave, beckoning to her. 'I've found it. Gold!'

She ran up the slope to join him and stood and stared, breathlessly, at the chunks of sparkling grey clay he held in his hands. 'Are you sure? It's not fool's gold?'

'This is the real stuff,' he yelled at her, excitedly. 'There's plenty more of it. You were right to tell me to hang on in here, gal.' He suddenly hugged hold of her and spun her around in his arms. 'If you ask me, we're rich.'

Alice's face lit up and she, too, shrieked with joy as he whirled her around. It was not an unpleasant sensation being held by him, feeling his strength and warmth, but she gradually eased herself out of his grasp. 'Calm down. What are we going to do?'

'We're gonna have a damn good time once we git the gold outa this clay. We're gonna go down to Belinda's an' celebrate. Whiskey and cee-gars for everyone, that's what it'll be, wash some of this dirt outa my throat.'

'Be serious,' she said. 'You don't want to go mad until you know how much there is. Shouldn't we keep quiet about this for a while? We don't want the whole world rushing up here.'

'They'll be outa luck. This is the last claim there is, 'less they wanna climb up and claim the cliff face. Hey, maybe you'd better register a separate claim on that yourself.'

'Perhaps I should,' she agreed.

Hillside claims were something new in the Yukon. Gold was believed to exist only in the beds of creeks. But what the prospectors did not realize was that in some places a more ancient creek bed existed than one which was visible. Geological upheaval had buried and hidden these. Such was the case here. After blasting through solid rock they had hit a strand of soft grey shale flecked with black iron and sparkling gold dust. Scope climbed through the narrow entranceway of his hole and Alice ducked down after him to take a look. 'All we gotta do,' he grunted, as he lit a candle, 'is follow this seam.'

'Good Lord!' Alice exclaimed, as she examined a glittering chunk of clay in her palm. 'It's easy, isn't it?'

★ ★ ★

It was almost unbelievable. They were washing out gold worth $100 to the pan. After two weeks of digging and sluicing they were running out of containers to keep the dust. Scope rode into Dawson with a bottle of it to check it out and returned with good news. It was top quality and he had $2,000 in cash paid by the Wells Fargo office. 'What 'n hell's the rest of it gonna be worth?' he asked.

Gold and cash aplenty was no use, however, if there was nothing to buy. Supplies in Skagway were getting short. He had managed to get some sacks of flour, sugar, beans and oats at sky-high prices. But if they were to get through the winter to work the mine it was time to think about stocking up on fish, meat, root vegetables and berries to see them through.

'What are you doing?' Alice asked, when she saw him digging a hole six feet square and five deep outside the cabin. 'Looking for more gold?'

'Nope. Making a safe for the food.'

He lined the hole with flat stones he found in the creek, knocking them firm into the walls. When the first frosts came he would leave it open to freeze hard. 'It's a kinda ice-house. Gimme them bilberries you dried.' He placed the sack of dried fruit in a corner. 'That'll be the first of our store.'

For the time being he covered the hole with stakes weighted down by more flat stones and camouflaged it with pine needle brush. 'That should keep any nosy varmints out. C'mon, gal, it's time to hit the saloon.'

Alice could no longer refuse. Their future appeared to be assured. So she tried to titivate herself, putting on her clean blouse with cameo brooch, her spare skirt and the new stockings he had brought her from town.

Scope was consumed with a shudder of desire as he saw her smooth the hosiery on her shapely legs and fix them with garters. A flash of white thigh made him groan almost with pain. 'Jeezis!' he moaned, as he went outside.

'What's she doing to a guy?'

Already the blustery wind had an icy feel and there was a sprinkling of snow on the ground as they rode two-up on Rajah down to Grand Forks, spending some of their dust, smiling at the secret of their bond. It so happened the sergeant of redcoats, Jim, was making a call and he joined them in their corner of the candle-flickering bar room.

His news was that Florence was prospering buying and selling gold, that the two paddle steamers had moved out north before the Yukon River froze solid, and that there was considerable concern that there could be a winter of starvation. Beseiged by demands from the 3,000 Klondikers in Dawson City the warehouses were running out of supplies and had already started rationing their goods.

MacArthur was well spoken and knowledgeable and was telling Alice that he was a native of England and hoped to make a career in the service. The girl appeared to have only eyes and ears for the tall officer and was chatting with him avidly about places like London and Montreal and people Scope had barely heard of.

She was telling him, too, about her life in New York and how her father had run into big financial trouble during the past three years' nationwide slump. 'He has debts of fifty thousand dollars, mostly owed to friends of the family. I feel honour bound to try to repay them,' she said. 'That's why I'm here.'

This was not something she had ever mentioned to Scope and he felt peeved, especially when the redcoat patted her hand and replied, 'I admire you for that, Alice.'

Scope was feeling as randy as hell and almost inclined to get his oats with Carrot Top Gert, or even Ear-biter Ethel. But he had imbibed a bit too freely of Belinda's corn liquor and was thirsting for a fight instead. He shouldered his way to the bar, chatted to a couple of the calico queens, and lurched back to say, brusquely, 'Come on, gal. It's time you an' me were getting back.'

Alice smiled apologetically at Jim and whispered, 'I hope you don't get the wrong idea about this.'

The mountie got to his feet and saluted. 'What you do is entirely your business, Alice.'

'Yes it is,' she cried, angrily brushing Scope off when he tried to take her arm. 'What's the hurry?'

Outside she turned on him, pulling herself away from his grasp. 'How could you be so rude? You don't own me.'

Scope climbed unsteadily on to Rajah and put out his hand. 'Git up here, Alice, 'less you wanna walk.'

Reluctantly she allowed him to swing her up to sit behind him, but tried not to touch him, hanging precariously on to the cantle instead as he set off at a fast lope. 'You're drunk,' she scolded. 'I don't like you like this.'

Back at the cabin he caught hold of her waist and stared at her. 'You make me jealous. Those ain't good feelings to stir up in a man.'

'Jealous? Of Jim? You've no cause to be. He's just a friend. Nor have you any right to be jealous of me. You promised — '

'Promised? Yeah, I did.' He held her tighter, his face tense with anger. 'But bad things can come of jealousy.' He pushed her away, contemptuously, and went to attend to the horse, calling back, 'Don't worry, li'l Miss Goody Two Shoes. Your virtue's intact with me.'

* * *

He was not feeling too proud of himself the next morning, his head pounding with a foul hangover, and was somewhat pleased when Skookum Jim arrived and suggested he join him for a jaunt over the divide to visit his relatives. 'We should be able to stock up on supplies,' Skookum said, 'before the snows set in.'

Scope was silent as he saddled the

horse and packed his rifle in his blanket roll. Alice came out to watch him. 'How long will you be gone?' she asked.

'Dunno,' he said, sounding surly. 'Maybe a few days. You stay here. Jim's gonna borrow the mule to ride.'

'Can't I come?'

'Nope.' He shook his head as he tightened the cinch. 'You'd slow us up. It ain't woman country out there.'

However, he removed the revolver from his holster and handed it to her. 'You hang on to this. Anybody comes nosin' round tell 'em to git in no uncertain fashion. You know how to shoot it? It needs a good strong pull. I'll leave you Kai and the team, too. They'll protect ya.'

'You better bring along that keg of corn whiskey from Belinda's and that sack of Bull Durham, too,' Jim said. 'It'll come in handy to trade.'

'Sure.' Scope tied the whiskey behind the saddle. He had planned to imbibe it himself, but maybe best not.

He swung aboard and set off down

the creek, followed by Jim. Alice watched them go and felt forlorn that Scope did not shout 'So long' or turn in the saddle to wave.

'Men!' she exclaimed. 'They never grow up. I do hope he's not going to be difficult.'

8

Skookum Jim, his brother-in-law Tagish Charlie, and their salmon-fishing pal, George Washington Carmack, had been the first to discover Klondike gold when they had been nosing around Rabbit Creek the previous summer.

'At first nobody believed us,' Jim told Scope as they rode along. 'When we started bringing in pouches of dust they sure did. The rush was on. That's when they renamed the creeks Bonanza and Eldorado and one after me.'

'So what happened? You don't look partic'larly wealthy?'

Skookum was wearing an ancient black overcoat, torn and sheened, a feather in his concertinaed top hat, buckskin leggings and moccasins. He shrugged and said, 'Wimmin, whiskey, false friends and cheatin' saloon 'keeps, it soon goes.'

'Yeah,' Scope muttered. 'I ain't gonna fritter mine away.'

Skookum Jim led him over the Divide, treacherous with first snow, and down into the vast tract of forest on the far side. The trail he followed would be invisible to all but an Indian or mountain sheep. They had to climb around wind-fallen trees and wade through boggy marsh so progress was slow, and they kept a wary eye out for grizzlies or black bears. But eventually they reached the Indian River without hindrance.

Scope could smell the Siwash encampment a mile before they reached it — but the same could be said of Dawson. The aroma here was of rancid salmon, for the Indians spent much time rendering fish-heads down into oil. They were a greasy-looking bunch, a strong Mongolian slant to their features. Their canoes were drawn up on the beach and they lived in a circle of cabins.

Amid a clamour of children and dogs Skookum Jim was greeted amiably. His name in their language meant Good Jim and although he didn't often visit he was warmly welcomed when he did. He put an arm around an Esquimaux-looking squaw in parka and buckskins and grinned. 'Here's my wife, Kate, an' them's my kids.'

When they had smoked and talked they got down to the business of trade. Scope gave the village headman a can of peaches as a gift, and traded his sugar for a pile of salmon that had been dried and smoked on racks. Although they had their own form of tobacco, growing wild, Bull Durham was always much in demand. He traded it for two bags of pemmican. This would keep for months in a cold climate.

Most of the Indian men had been turning their slant eyes eagerly towards the keg of whiskey. 'What am I bid?' Scope asked.

'One of 'em's offering his squaw for the night,' Skookum Jim drawled. 'She'll give you a good time.'

'It sure is tempting,' the American

replied, eyeing the comely young woman. 'But I'd rather have an outfit like she's got on.'

When this was translated, the squaw beamed broadly and ran off to her hut. She returned with a caribou parka with a fur-edged hood, mittens attached, and fringed leggings. 'Throw in a pair of fur boots and the whiskey's yourn,' Scope grinned.

The Siwash claimed the whiskey and immediately started passing it around. It was a privilege to him to be able to host a party. Soon the villagers were drumming, dancing, laughing and generally fooling and falling around as the keg went round.

Skookum Jim showed Scope a six-foot sled. 'They say you can have this for ten silver dollars. We'll drag it behind us on the way back. You start loading up. I got business with my squaw.'

He disappeared into a hut with Kate while Scope got ready to leave. He sat and smoked and drank with them as the night, lengthening now, slowly passed, wondering how long Jim would be. Suddenly he was shaking Scope's shoulder. 'C'mon, friend, let's get outa here 'fore things git nasty. These boys can't hold their liquor. Somebody's bound to get stabbed.'

They had a job disentangling themselves from the drunken and effusive Siwash. Finally they just jumped on their mounts and raced away along the riverbank, the mule going at a stiff-legged trot, braying his disgust as Jim belaboured him with a stick.

'We should be back by nightfall,' Skookum yelled. So, they would only have been away two days. Alice was going to be surprised . . .

★   ★   ★

Back in Skagway the flamboyant Jeff Smith had gotten bored with fleecing would-be Klondikers all summer. He had a hankering to see Dawson City for himself and maybe move in on the action there. So when the first snows fell in mid-September he locked up Jeff's Place, donned his big Stetson and black fox coat, and with six of his thugs portaging their baggage, set off on the Dalton trail. He hoped to reach the Lewes River running into the Yukon while there was still a free-flowing channel through the ice. Otherwise it would be one long walk.

When he reached Dawson, Soapy took a look around town and decided that the classiest joint was the Monte Carlo saloon and casino. It had been opened by 'Swiftwater' Bill Gates, who had made a fortune out of Unlucky Thirteen on the Eldorado, cleaning up $155,000 as his share the previous summer of '96.

The bearded, braggartly Swiftwater Bill was as flamboyant as Soapy himself, and had spared no expense on his saloon, importing a mahogany bar, chandeliers and roulette tables by barge. The barge had been stacked, too, with barrels of whiskey on which were sat as they floated into Dawson a bevy of beauties recruited in San Francisco.

Now the Monte Carlo was operating at full throttle, open day and night, the wheels of fortune spinning, the whiskey flowing and the so-called dancing girls operating in shifts to entertain the miners. The girls' take was never less than $30 a day, or night often more, and most had gold nuggets sewn into their belts, the grateful contributions of satisfied panhandlers.

'Looks to me like this place could keep us in clover,' Smith drawled to his new 'lieutenant', a clean-shaven Norwegian, Lars Lanson, as he took a sip of the whiskey and surveyed the boisterous scene. 'I'm gonna move in.'

'Ja.' Lanson flexed his brickhard muscles beneath his jersey. 'Good idea, boss.'

Soapy stood with his rifle under his arm and a revolver stuck in his belt and watched the five foot six Swiftwater Bill, in his cutaway coat, gold-threaded waistcoat, and diamond stickpin in his cravat, strolling around supervising proceedings.

'Tell that little fat loud mouth I want words with him,' he snapped at the bar-keep. 'Pronto, you hear?'

When the 'keep called him across, Swiftwater Bill arrived, his face creased in a smile, rubbing his pudgy hands, saying, 'Good evening, gentlemen, can I help you?'

'Yeah,' Smith replied. 'How much do you make outa this joint in a week? Two thousand dollars? Ten thousand?'

'That is my business,' Bill said. 'But I'm doing OK. Why should you want to know?'

'Because I'm taking sixty per cent of it.'

'What?'

'Me an' my boys are moving in to help you run the joint and give you protection. You may well need it. Ain't that so, Lars?'

'Ja.' The Norwegian bunched his right fist, cracking the knuckles, and slammed Swiftwater a piledriver to the jaw. 'We're the best there is, see?'

He was addressing Bill who had gone down as if poleaxed and was lying on the boards shaking his head.

'Never,' Bill mumbled, spitting blood. 'You ain't having my saloon.'

Lars booted him heftily in the side. 'Mister,' he glowered. 'It ain't wise to argue.'

He picked up a roulette table with massive strength and hurled it over the mahogany bar to crash into the mirrored backshelf of glasses and bottles.

As the 'keep brought out a revolver, Smith clouted him across the jaw with his rifle, making him spit a shower of teeth. 'Naughty!' he cautioned. 'We don't want anyone shot, do we? At least not just yet.'

Other of Bill Gates's minions moved in to help him as he climbed to his knees, so Soapy jerked his head at his other enforcers. 'Go get 'em, boys.'

Clubs, brass knuckles suddenly appeared, the professional thugs making mincemeat of the Monte Carlo staff, beating them back, mercilessly. All bedlam broke loose as the girls screamed. Most of the miners joined in the affray, not really knowing who they were hitting or why, just taking a swipe at the first face that appeared in the scrum.

A Chinese cook ran from the kitchen a meat cleaver in his hand. Smith caught him a klonk with his rifle as Lanson grabbed hold of him and tossed him over the bar to join the 'keep.

Eventually, Soapy fired his revolver into the air and the scrimmage slowly wound to a halt. 'That's enough,' he yelled. 'This is just to let you know I'm the new management of this place. Drinks on the house, boys and girls.'

He looked around for Swiftwater Bill but he had disappeared. 'Where's that ratbag gone?'

Lars grinned at him. 'I guess he's headed back to Seattle.'

* * *

Alice had been busy at the cabin while Scope was away, cutting up canvas she

139

had originally intended to use as a tent and sewing it into foot-long bags. These she was carefully filling with the flecks of gold from the saucepans and empty cans they had used as containers, pulling the drawstrings tight, and packing them on their raft of logs. She was turning it over in her mind whether to ask for her cut and return to Dawson City. She was not sure she could face the long winter cooped up in the cabin with the lusty young American. It was not fair on him and, frankly, it was not fair on her, either. A woman was not devoid of sexual urges, but in that society it was imperative they had to be controlled, or she might well be ruined.

It was quite a surprise that morning when she heard the clink of a bridle and a horse snorting with effort as it climbed up the creek. Her first thought was that it was Scope returned, but when she got to her feet a bolt of fear hit her. The rider was Frenchie Pete and with him were the four *voyageurs*.

For moments Alice froze, then she

turned and ran as fast as her long skirts allowed towards the cabin. She could hear the horse pounding after her and as she reached to open the door a knife thudded into the woodwork pinning her by her tight-waisted jacket to it.

'Got her!' grinned Couteau. He had hurled his pig-sticker from thirty feet. 'Good throw, huh?'

'Yeah, we sure got her this time,' Pete gloated. 'An' she's all on her li'l own.'

Alice tried to wriggle out of her jacket and screamed, 'Kai! Get him.'

The husky raced towards Couteau and hurled himself at his throat but the Frenchman pulled a chain from his pocket and beat him off. He used all his strength to hit the dog across the head and Kai whimpered and rolled away to lay senseless.

The rest of the pack did not have Kai's courage and backed as Couteau set about them with the chain. 'Yes, you bastards. You soon learn who's boss. We get a pretty price for you.'

Meanwhile Pete had jumped down

and caught Alice by the throat, staring into her grey eyes. 'Well, my little cherub. What you do now?'

For answer she spat in his face and he back-handed her viciously, knocking her into the dust. 'This baby's really asking for it.'

'*Oui*,' Couteau growled. 'Let's have her.'

'She's yours, my friend.' Pete was more interested in taking a look at the mine and when he strode across and saw the bags of gold dust lined up on the raft he gave a whistle of awe. 'They been busy. There must be twenty thousand dollar here.'

The dark-skinned *voyageur* in the red wool hat kneeled down beside him. 'Ah,' he gloated. 'We are rich. How kind of them.'

'Yes, Jean,' Pete instructed. 'Let's get it packed into that tarpaulin sheet and tied to the horse ready for a quick getaway.'

He had stolen the mustang in Dawson, one of only a dozen horses available in the town. It was a wornout, knock-kneed hack but it would serve.

The squat Couteau had hoisted Alice to her feet and pushed her into the cabin. He swung his chain, threateningly, as she faced him, defiantly. 'You want it easy, missy, or what?'

'Keep away from me,' she warned. 'You wouldn't dare. The redcoats will hang you.'

He hit her a blow in the face with the chain and Alice screamed, struggling as he threw her down on to the bed of pine brush. His ugly frog-like face was smirking at her distress as he tore apart her bolero and bodice and her pale breasts spilled free. Couteau gripped her hair in his fist and set to biting maniacally at her nipples. With his other hand he tried to restrain her kicking legs. He pulled up her skirt and petticoat and wrested them apart.

'Vairy nice,' he panted, dragging apart his own clothing and striving to pull himself into her.

'Get off me, you filthy beast.' He had

her pinned down and was grunting and sweating as he pumped at her. Alice turned her head away in desperation and tried to reach under the bedding for the triple action. She found the barrel, swung it out and cracked him across the head, pummelling at him until he slumped unconscious.

'Get off me,' she repeated, hurling him from her, as another of the thugs appeared in the doorway. In a panic she caught hold of the butt of the Iver Johnson and waved it at him. 'Keep away, I'm warning you.'

But the Frenchman took a step towards her. A good hard pull. Alice remembered Scope's words. It seemed to take an age to fire the revolver. But an explosion crashed out and the man toppled back out of the door clutching at a bloody hole in his chest. 'You bitch,' he groaned. 'Why you do thees?'

Scope was almost home. One hundred yards from the cabin he heard the screams and the pistol shot; it was as if for moments all the life seeped from his body as he rode Rajah up the creek. 'Oh, God! No!' he moaned.

He vaulted from the horse as the crack of a rifle, sending a bullet whistling past his ear, informed him that Frenchie Pete intended to kill him. He could see him standing by the bluff of rock by the mine. Scope pulled the horse into cover and slid his Marlin Ballard ten-shot rifle from the blanket roll. He levered it and took a quick pop at the Frenchman.

He missed by an inch as Pete backed away, returning fire, to disappear behind the bluff. Without hesitation Scope raced up the hill. It was suicidal, he knew, but what else could he do? He was faced by a man in a red wool hat who hurled an axe at him. Scope ducked as it nearly parted his hair and fired his second slug.

'Aagh!' Jean groaned as he rolled away to lie still as a shot rabbit.

Scope levered the rifle and put another in Jean's back to make sure. But he had to dive for cover in the bushes as Frenchie Pete and another man in a fur hat sent a fusillade of rifle and revolver fire his way.

Alice had reached the doorway of the cabin, leaning against it, raising the Iver Johnson to aim it in her trembling hands at Frenchie Pete's back. But as she did so Couteau came round, somewhat groggily, and his knife thudded into Alice's shoulder. She gasped and collapsed, sliding to the ground, losing hold of the revolver.

'Got her!' Couteau shouted, pulling his knife from her back and hurriedly stepping over her. 'Looks like Roland's dead.'

'So's Jean,' Pete shouted. 'Where's that bastard got to?'

There was no sign of the American who had wriggled his way up through the scrub of felled pines aiming to get behind them, unsure how many were left. However, when he got to his feet and made a run up the slope Frenchie Pete swung his Mauser and a lucky shot smashed into Scope's thigh like a sledge-hammer blow, knocking his legs from under him. All he could do was sink down behind a log and grit his teeth against a nausea of pain.

Now it was just a matter of time before the three Frenchmen found him. Or was it? If he could drag himself over the slope behind the cabin . . . gasping with pain he worked his way out of the brush as they searched, shouting that they would kill him.

'You gotta find me first,' he muttered, as he slid into his cold store hole.

'*Ou est il*?' he heard one call and, forcing himself to his feet, he poked the rifle out and saw the 'fur hat' one prowl past. One squeeze of the trigger sent him spinning into eternity.

'He's got Michel!' Frenchie Pete spun around with alarm and shouted at Couteau, 'Let's get out of here.'

Both men, puzzled by where the shot had come from, backed away, retreating over the brow of the hill. Pete jumped on the mustang. 'Giddap!' he yelled, and went charging wildly down the creek, the roped raft of gold dust bouncing along behind.

'Wait for me!' Couteau shouted, finding Rajah and galloping after him.

When he split up with Scope at the foot of the creek Skookum Jim had intended to ride the mule along to Belinda's place. When he heard the gunshots he turned back. 'What's going on?' he wondered. When he saw Frenchie Pete coming hell for leather towards him he took cover in the woods, not sure what to do. But as Pete went past he saw one of the sacks of gold bounce out and spill on the trail.

'He's stole their dust,' Skookum shouted, in two minds whether to go after him, or return to see how his friends had fared. He unhitched his shotgun from the saddle horn and, as he moved the mule back on to the trail, came face to face with Couteau.

The little Frenchman slowed the running Rajah with his left hand and Skookum saw that he had a blood-stained knife in his right and he was raising it to hurl his way. Skookum Jim did not hesitate. He jerked up his twelve gauge and gave him a bellyful of shot. Couteau was bowled out of the saddle, squealing like a stuck pig. When the second barrel peppered his chest he fell back dead.

'That settled his hash,' Skookum muttered and kicked heels into the mule, charging back up the creek.

'What 'n tarnation's bin goin' on?' he exclaimed when he saw Alice lying sprawled face down on the ground, a dark patch of blood oozing from the back of her dress. Nearby were the bodies of three *voyageurs* laid in postures of death.

He jumped down from the mule as Scope crawled from his hole, clutching his bloody thigh. Skookum Jim knelt beside the girl, turning her over, staring at her ripped clothes, her bitten, naked breasts, her bruised and bloodstreaked face. 'She's still breathin',' he said, 'but it don't look good.'

9

Jeff Smith had lined up all the girls before him in the Monte Carlo. 'Here's how it's gonna be,' he told them, pulling back his fox fur coat to reveal the revolver in his belt. 'Now I'm taking charge of this joint you're all gonna have to take a pay cut. From what I hear you've had it easy too long. From here on there won't be no basic wage. You'll just get thirty per cent of whatever the customer pays. Any li'l extras they donate will have to be handed over to the management.'

'That's not fair.' A buxom little body known as Georgeous Gussie tossed her wig's golden ringlets and faced him, eyes blazing. 'In fact, it's downright crazy.'

'Life ain't fair, sweetheart.' Smith smiled at her in his oily fashion, his eyes cold as the temperature outside — it had already fallen to zero. 'But unless you want my boys to rearrange them pretty features of yourn you'll do as I say. Right, let's get on with the party. Start them wheels spinning. Hit the keys, Mr Piano Player. What y'all looking so glum about?'

Gussie turned to the other girls, clenched her fists, her arms akimbo. 'I ain't working for those terms. I'm going on strike. Girls, who's with me?'

'Right,' Jeff sighed, jerking his head at Lanson. 'It's time we showed her the door. I've tried to be nice, but she won't listen. Kick the li'l cow out into the cold, Lars, and make sure nobody else'll wanna employ her.'

He had spent half an hour clearing up the broken glass and toppled chairs after the scrimmage and was keen to take over the Monte Carlo and start making some cash.

But as Lanson advanced on Gussie, grabbing her by the throat, his hand raised to give her a slap, the saloon swing doors were pushed open and

Sergeant Jim MacArthur stepped inside. 'That's enough!'

As he spoke two other redcoats came in, one through the side door and another by way of the kitchen, and they had rifles at the ready in their hands.

Swiftwater Gates poked his bearded and bruised face through the front doors and pointed at Soapy. 'There he is! That's the crazy sonuvabitch. Look at what he's done to my beautiful saloon. Look at the mirrors; look at the glass; look what he done to my face.'

Smith's five henchmen spun around, their hands reaching in their pockets for weapons, ready for a fight. Lanson still had Gussie by the throat, his hand raised. But Soapy let his coat drop back over his gunbutt and said, ingratiatingly, 'What's he on about, Officer? It's him who attacked us.'

'You liar,' Swiftwater yelled, coming inside, but cowering behind MacArthur. 'Look, he was about to beat up poor Gussie.'

'Yeah, the big stiff,' she shouted,

taking the opportunity to kick the Norwegian in the crotch, then backing off. 'He wanted us to take a paycut. The nerve of the man!'

'I'm prepared to overlook your ingratitude, Gates,' Soapy told the saloon-keep, 'an' come to an amicable arrangement with you privately. No need to trouble the gentlemen of the law with this. We can still be partners. How about sixty-forty in your favour?'

'Get lost,' Swiftwater roared, taking Gussie under his arm to console her. 'You stick with me, sweetie. Arrest them, Officer. I'm prepared to bring charges of assault.'

'Shut up, the lot of you,' Jim snapped. 'Let's have some order in here. Right, first, all of you men, hand over your arms.'

When his thugs protested, Smith shrugged and offered his revolver. 'Anything to oblige you brave boys, although this is an infringement of our liberties. Do as he says, *mes amis*.'

Several more mounties had arrived,

part of a contingent dispatched from Winnipeg following the wholesale desertions from Fort Cudahy. Eager to show their keeness they shoved Smith and his cohorts into a corner of the saloon and began manacling them with irons on their wrists and ankles.

'You can't do this to me,' Soapy whined. 'I'm a respected businessman in Skagway.'

'Yeah,' Jim replied. 'I've heard about you. That's where you're going back to. We don't want your kind in Canada.'

He turned a deaf ear to Smith's demands to see a lawyer. 'Put 'em on the log pile today, men. Tomorrow you can escort them on the five hundred mile march back to Alaska. It'll give you a chance to see the country.'

'You can't do that,' Soapy cried. 'This is downright inhuman. It's blowing a blizzard outside.'

'Too bad.' Jim McArthur had been brought in as second in command at Dawson City. Fort Selkirk and the post on the border at Chilcoot Pass would need reinforcements so they would kill two birds with one stone, so to speak. 'If the USA has no interest in enforcing law and order in Alaska, that doesn't apply this side of the border. Take this scumbag away and make sure he does some work.'

★ ★ ★

Skookum Jim had used an old Indian recipe to treat Alice's wound, using a poultice of moss and herbs and bandaging it tight across her back. But blood soon began to leak from the deep knife wound and he shook his head. 'I done all I can for her. I gotta take her into the hospital at Dawson. I'll harness the sled to the horse. It's gonna be rough going for thirty miles. I hope she can take it.'

The girl was drifting in and out of consciousness for she had lost a lot of blood. Scope lay on the cold ground clutching his own wound, looking on helplessly. He nodded. 'I guess it's the only hope.'

Alice's eyes fluttered open and she murmured, 'What happened to the gold?'

'Aw, that first fella, Frenchie Pete, he had it slung on your work raft. It's all gawn,' Jim said.

Alice met Scope's eyes. 'I'm sorry, I shouldn't have — '

'Doncha worry about that, Alice. Your life's more important to me than gold. Main thang's to git you well. I should nevuh have left ya alone. Jim's right. Father Judge and the nuns of St Anne will take good care of you.'

When Skookum Jim had wrapped her in her overcoat, blanket, hat and muffler and tied her to the seat of the sled, he went to help Scope hop into the cabin. 'That wound don't look good,' he grunted, as he washed it and gave it the same Indian treatment, binding the poultice with a torn-up shirt.

'It don't feel good,' Scope replied,

with a grimace of agony. 'But at least his slug passed right through.'

'Nah, I can't see no splinters of bone!'

'A pity I gave that whiskey away. I could sure do with a slug.'

'You just rest in here. Keep the fire going. Main thing's not to git cold. Pneumonia soon sets in.'

'Yeah,' Scope agreed. 'And gangrene.'

Both men knew he had only a fifty-fifty chance of pulling through without having to have the limb amputated. The prospect off being a one-legged cripple was not very appealing, but Scope forced a grin and whispered, 'I'll be OK. Thanks, Skookum. You go look after Alice.'

'Sure.' Jim poked some logs into the stove and tugged his Lincoln hat firmly over his brow. 'I'll see yuh in coupla days.'

He went outside, shouted at Rajah to go, hung on to the back of the sled and tried to guide it as gently as he could down the slope. But as Alice groaned with pain he knew it was going to be a rough ride and possibly a futile one.

★　★　★

When they had gone Scope suddenly remembered Kai. Fighting nausea and a head-spinning dizziness he used his rifle as a crutch to go back out to look for him. The husky was lying on his side and for moments Scope's heart seemed to stop as he thought he was dead. He peered at him and bent to stroke his head, noticing blood at the back of his head matting the silver-blue fur. Suddenly Kai whimpered and looked his way as if saying, 'Sorry, master, I don't feel so good.' The chain had hit him hard.

'Come on, boy,' Scope coaxed, and as he headed back to the cabin Kai clambered to his feet and tottered after him. 'Come into the warm. You'll be OK.' In spite of an urgent desire to collapse on to his bed, Scope first sought a side of bacon, carved chunks and tossed it out to the rest of the dogs who, of course, slept outside. He bit into a piece himself and tried to coax Kai to eat but the husky just shook his head and dumbly refused.

'Waal, that's unusal for you, ain't it?' Scope said, sinking with relief back on to his feather bag. 'Come on.' He patted his side. 'Come an' keep me warm, pal.'

Kai groaned and crawled over, resting his head on Scope's chest, snuggling close. 'You'll be OK, boy,' Scope said. 'We all will.' But he wasn't so sure.

★   ★   ★

From the scorching sunshine of the summer days suddenly the winter had descended upon them. It was only late October but already the days were shortening dramatically. Soon there would only be a brief couple of hours of glimmering daylight as darkness took over the land. If you lived fifty miles below the Arctic circle it was only to be expected. But most of the cheechakos who had made the pilgrimage of greed for riches were unprepared for such changes in the northern land. Already the rivers had frozen hard and the two paddle steamers which had headed north had found they had left it too late. The ice closed in and trapped them and there they would be stuck for six months. Their captains, crew and passengers, who were hoping to get back to 'civilization', had to abandon ship and trek through a snowstorm to Fort Cudahy to seek refuge.

Jeff Smith and his thugs took a dim view of things as they were herded by a group of redcoats along the freezing river and set out on the long trek back to Alaska. Soapy cursed the mounties, the weather, Swiftwater Bill, everybody and anybody as he struggled back towards Skagway. 'Why,' he moaned, 'did I ever leave my nice warm saloon? I must have been crazy.' Before them was thirty or forty days, at least, maybe longer, braving the tempests. They would be lucky not to lose fingers or toes to frostbite.

'Aw, quit moaning,' one of the redcoats said, as they huddled around their camp-fire one night. 'Who invited you to come here in the first place?' The only good thing, as far as Smith was concerned, was that at least the snow was not yet deep enough to slow them right down. But, as he eyed the gloomy clouds scurrying over them through the night sky, he knew as well as any man that a blizzard could strike them at any time.

* * *

The dogs barking frenziedly woke Scope from a half-doze he had drifted into. Kai's nape fur bristled as he gave a deep growl. 'Now what's happening?' The wounded man gritted his teeth against the pain as he tried to get up from his bed. He leaned on his rifle as he hopped over to unlatch the door. The tethered dogs were kicking up a

161

horrendous din, leaping about with fear and excitement. Scope followed the direction of their gaze and saw through the twilight a huge hairy beast dragging something away up the slope into the trees.

Suddenly he realized that the Frenchman Alice had shot, whom Jim had moved ten feet away from the cabin had disappeared. He shouldered the Ballard, wobbling on his one good leg and fired at the retreating grizzly. At that range in the dim twilight it was a difficult shot. He did not want to wound it or enrage it, just scare it off. So he sent two more bullets in its general direction. 'That's the biggest damn grizzly I've seen,' he gritted out.

When he had quietened the dogs he went to take a look at the other two corpses. The 'fur hat' one lay untouched, but the 'sock-hat' one was badly mauled. Their dead weight in his present state was too much for him to move. When Skookum returned they would have to toss them into a nearby gully. 'It's a bad business,' he said to Kai when he got back to the cabin. 'Now that grizzly's got a taste for human flesh he'll no doubt be back sometime to finish his breakfast.'

He examined the wound in his right thigh above the knee, grimaced at the torn flesh and nerves, and, sickened, eased himself back on to his bunk. It was going to be a long, lonely wait.

★   ★   ★

For centuries Jesuit priests had been sent from France to North America, going out into the deepest wilderness, suffering horrendous tortures and 'martyrdoms' in their bid to convert the heathens. The native Indians for their part were somewhat averse to giving up their own religions. A few of the priests succeeded in making their mark through amazing selflessness and willpower. Such a one was Father

Judge, who had been in the Yukon many years. He followed the stampeders knowing that disease and trouble would be their lot. He built a cabin chapel, which unfortunately burned down when he knocked over a candle falling asleep at his prayers.

The Klondikers dug deep in their pockets and built him another, installing an imported organ, too. They organized an annual membership of the new hospital that was raised in Dawson City. Membership cost three ounces of dust. Joined in the summer of '97 by the nursing order of the Sisters of St Anne, Father Judge now presided over a modern three-storey hospital block. He worked all hours feeding, treating and often burying his flock.

'He feeds ya beans, gives ya the medicine, then prays for ya,' was the saying in Dawson that summer. 'He's the one true Christian in this city.'

It was there Skookum Jim arrived with his horse sled. The nuns, known by the Indians as Black Robes, ran out to help carry Alice inside and lay her on a pallet. The elderly priest examined her and said, 'The Lord has been kind. The knife stab was deflected by her shoulder blade. However, whoever perpetrated this act gave the knife a nasty twist before he pulled it out. He did not intend this young woman to live.'

'Nah,' Skookum growled, 'an' I didn't intend him to live when I shotgunned him.'

'What went on?' one of the nuns enquired.

'I ain't sure,' Jim replied, 'but I got the feelin' she was badly abused by them varmints 'fore they stole her gold. Treat her gentle, Sister. I figure she's hurt in her mind as much as in her body.'

'We will look after her,' the nun assured him. 'But perhaps you should report this to the redcoats.'

'Yeah, guess I should, not that I like havin' much to do with them boys. They tax ya as soon as ya talk.'

However, Sergeant Jim MacArthur

seemed more than upset by Skookum's tale. 'You say there's four dead up there?'

'That's right. One I shotgunned myself. Another two Scope put down 'fore they got him. And one I'm pretty sure Alice took out herself. 'Course, it was obvious it was self-defence. Hate to think what they were trying to do to that poor gal.'

MacArthur twisted his mouth in agitation. 'I'd better come up and take a look at the bodies. First I've got to go to the hospital to see if Alice is all right.'

'Didn't you oughta be gittin' after the one who got away? Frenchie Pete they call him. I reckon he's headed back to Skagway. He was the leader of that bunch of skunks. An' he's stolen twenty thousand in dust.'

'You're right. I've met that character. I'll alert my men for the pursuit. He won't get far.'

'Yeah, maybe he will, maybe he won't. He knows this country. In my opinion your men are jest a load of greenhorns.'

* ★ ★

How many days she lay in a feverish coma Alice knew not, visited by strange dreams, trying to twist and rise and call out, restrained by the soothing arms of a nun. When she awoke one morning to find herself lying on a pallet in the women's ward she asked a passing nun, 'Where am I?'

'So, you're awake?' her nurse exclaimed. 'You're safe now. Are you able to sit up and take some broth?'

Florence came to visit her, wanting to know what had happened, but Alice was reluctant to discuss the details. She felt ashamed and soiled. Could she really have killed that man?

'Don't blame yourself,' Jim MacArthur told her. 'It was him or you. I've been up and took a look.'

'How is Scope?' The words tumbled out before she realized what she was saying. She feared the answer.

'He's OK,' Sergeant MacArthur assured her. 'He had a lucky escape, too. His leg's healing. Not long 'fore he should be on his feet. But' — he looked out of the window at snow silently falling — 'there's plenty that won't. It's already forty below.'

The redcoat pulled on his winter issue sealskin hat, with its ear-muffs, and a heavy topcoat. 'If you've any sense you'll winter here in Dawson, Alice. That cabin's no place for you.'

'That's exactly what I've been telling her,' Florence put in. 'She can stay with me, become a partner in the business. I could do with the company.'

'But' — Alice bit her lower lip in a worried way — 'he'll be waiting for me. He's my partner. Business partner, I mean.'

'He'll be better able to manage on his own.' Jim rose and pulled on his gloves. 'Anyway, I gotta go.'

Alice reached out and squeezed his hand. 'Thanks for coming, Jim.'

A slight prickle of embarrassment speckled the redcoat's ruddy, shaven features. 'It weren't duty: I'm concerned about you, Alice. You're special to me.'

Florence watched him go. 'That's the man you ought to take up with. A fine, upstanding, responsible fellow. Not that nondescript cowboy, living in a hovel in the backwoods.'

'He's not a cowboy. He's a hunter and guide.'

'Alice, you're an educated New Yorker. The man is an ignorant drifter. He's not of your class. What possibly can you have in common, intellectually? Surely, nothing whatsoever.'

'He's educated in his own way, the only way that counts in these parts. He knows things you and I would never dream of about how to stay alive.'

'Huh! A lot of good backwoods' lore would be in New York. You *are* going back home, aren't you?'

'Of course,' Alice quickly replied. 'But I wish you wouldn't talk about Scope like that.'

'Scope! Even the name's absurd.

You're coming to spend the winter with me. There's no argument about it. I'll hear no more nonsense.'

Alice frowned and sighed. 'I'm very tired. I think I'll sleep now. But I suppose you're both right.'

★   ★   ★

There was panic in Dawson City. The Alaska Commercial Company's warehouses were dangerously low on supplies. The sternwheelers from the north couldn't get through due to the sudden fall in the river, the ice closing in, leaving only a narrow channel. The few that did were raided by gangs of armed men, demanding goods and paying for them at rifle point. The mounties had to be called in to guard the stores beseiged by angry miners. The Dominion Government offered free passage out to the safety of Fort Yukon in the far north. But the last two steamships to leave Dawson, loaded with refugees, got stuck fast on mudbanks. The marooned travellers were forced to walk through blizzards to the fort. Some died. All were badly frozen.

Florence Farthing had had the foresight to lay in stocks of flour, dried beans, blankets and baking powder, guessing they might become scarce. But as restaurants closed for lack of anything to serve and forcible rationing was introduced, she decided she had better hang onto what she had. She could have sold the salt for its weight in gold, literally.

'There's not a safety pin to be had in the whole town,' she said when she took Alice back to her neat cabin. 'I'm sorry it's so dark in here but glass windows are a thing of the past.'

'It's all right,' Alice murmured, still feeling weak and strangely shaken by her experiences. 'It's very nice, kind of you.' She was shivering with cold, stunned by the sudden transition from steaming summer to freezing winter.

'You lie down,' the sharp-nosed

Florence instructed. 'We'll have to share the bed. It's all I have. Would you believe I paid fourteen dollars for this broom? It was the last one going. I had to fight for it.'

People were leaving in droves in an effort to hike back through the blizzards to Skagway. Many wouldn't make it. No official count was ever made of how many lost their lives. Some were shipwrecked and drowned in their flimsy craft going up the coast or capsizing in the rivers' rapids. Others fell through ice or succumbed to dysentery, scurvy, consumption, malaria or sheer exhaustion, the slow freeze to death, and were lost in the snow. Thousands had turned back. Of the 30,000 who set out only 5,000 now remained alive in Dawson. The busiest men were the undertakers, ceaselessly driving dog-sled hearses up to the town cemetery.

Back in the USA a lot of hot air was spouted about the need to send relief to the starving miners. Funds were set up. But all that transpired was a crack-brained idea to transport a shipload of reindeer from Norway. Of the 530 animals only 144 remained alive by the time they reached Seattle. Their Lapland herders, too, had been decimated by measles. Only a handful of the men and beasts reached Skagway where nobody was sure what to do with them. The dark months of '97-'98 would come to be known as 'the starvation winter'.

The Indian half of Skookum Jim must have got the better of him because he didn't return for two weeks. By then Scope was feeling a lot improved. Nonetheless he was glad to see Jim on Rajah with the sled bouncing along behind. Scope hobbled out on a makeshift crutch to greet him. 'How's Alice? Where is she?'

'She'll pull through.' Jim had stayed longer than he intended in Dawson because there was still whiskey in the barrels in the saloons, if not much else. He had brought a jug of corn liquor with him and waved it, triumphantly. 'Brought ya somethang to warm your bones, Scope. Cain't say I don't think of ya.'

They sat by the stove and passed the jug, the fiery brew, indeed, sending a sensation of warmth through the body. 'Bull Durham's up to five dollars a sack,' Jim said, stuffing his pipe and tossing the tobacco across. 'Cigars are impossible to git. It's unbelievable. The Alaska Company's ekeing out its supplies like misers. Personally I figure it's all a trick to send prices soaring.'

'When's she coming back?' Scope persisted. 'Alice — '

'Aw, ye'd better fergit about her, young fella. She's moved in with that skinny baggage — what's she called, Florence. They're OK, snug as two peas in a pod. No, boy, she won't be coming back. That gal's had her fill of wilderness ways.'

Scope pondered these words with a stab of bitterness in him as Skookum rambled on about a bull moose he'd seen on the far side of the divide. 'I'll go after him in the mornin'. I don't intend to starve. There's a thousand pounds of meat on that critter.'

'I'll come with you. You'll need more than a shotgun,' Scope said. 'I got salmon and pemmican stashed away, but we'll be needing fresh meat to last the winter. That's if you don't mind sharin' him, Jim.'

Scope wondered why he had said 'we'. He was on his own now. It was probably for the best that she stayed in Dawson.

'You ain't in no fit state to tackle the pass. I was gonna give you half if you lent me the rifle.'

'No, I'm OK. I've been packing ice on the wound. Damn cold, but it's done the trick. It's healed up well. I need to git out, to see some action. I been cooped up in here too long.'

'How's the dawg?'

'He's OK, too. He got a hefty blow with that chain across the back of his neck, but I guess his fur took the brunt of it.'

Jim took a swig and passed the jug across. 'What you gonna do about the horse? They're putting 'em all down in Dawson, what few there are. Eating 'em or selling 'em as dog meat. There's no fodder or corn to be had. Men figure they'd never last the winter through.'

'Yeah?' Scope stroked his shaven jowls. He didn't believe in beards. They could freeze solid in the night and suffocate a man. 'I shoulda laid in some hay, some of that red-tipped grass in the valley, but I didn't have time. No, I ain't gonna slaughter Rajah. I'd rather set him free, to fend for himself.'

Jim shook his head. 'He'll never make it. If the wolves don't git him, a cougar will.'

'The caribou survive by digging through the snow to the moss. Rajah will have to take his chances, too. I couldn't shoot him.' He smiled, apologetically. 'He's a pal of mine.'

Eventually the whiskey took its toll

and, after demonstrating a wild, whooping Indian dance, Skookum collapsed drunk on Alice's bed. Scope grinned and tossed a cover over him before turning in himself. If Alice wasn't coming back he had been thinking of inviting Skookum to be his partner. 'No way,' he muttered, 'if the smelly skunk's gonna snore all night like that.'

In the grey gloom of what passed now for a morning, for the sun did little but glimmer on the horizon, Scope got the excited dogs ready in front of the Indian sled. It was made of a light pine frame, its runners of curved ash, protected by brass skids rather than iron, which would split in the intense cold. The snow had settled nice and crisp. He would be able to hang on to the back and rest his gammy leg.

'Come on,' he shouted to Skookum, when he poked his head out of the cabin door. 'Let's be on our way. You ride Rajah. I'm leaving the saddle and harness behind so it'll have to be bareback.'

This was no problem to a half-Indian, and the older man snaked his lariat around the horse's jaws and jumped aboard. Well, not much of a problem apart from Skookum's thumping hangover.

They climbed steadily up to the divide past the icy Dome, the dogs eagerly taking it in their stride. At least, that was until they hit deep soft snow and started floundering. 'You'd better go first and beat us a way through,' Scope called.

Skookum glanced at him, wryly, but did so. Soon the gelding was up to his haunches, struggling valiantly. Suddenly he slipped and took a tumble, somersaulting over and sliding helplessly towards the edge of a cliff, his feet stuck up in the air, unable to right himself. Luckily, a boulder stopped him.

Skookum went arse over tip, as they say, to land beside the horse. He peered up, his tophat skew-whiff. 'Hot dang! Git me outa here.'

Scope pulled him out, then the two

men slid and tripped on the slope as they tried to heave the horse out of the drift. 'I told ya this was no country for a hoss,' Skookum yelled.

'We been through worse.' Scope busied himself with his knife scraping balled-up snow from the horse's hoofs once he was upright, 'But I see whacha mean. Let's try again. You better lead him with the rope.'

They got across the ridge and Scope was able to ride the sled again. It certainly was exhilarating to go skiing down the mountainside, shouting commands to Kai, the lead dog. 'Just like old times,' he said, when Jim joined him down in the pasture.

'Now I'll call up that bull moose.'

'You what?'

For answer Skookum put both hands over his mouth as if about to blow a raspberry, then made a long, low baying sound. He looked around and tried again. 'Ain't many men know this trick,' he beamed. 'That ol' moose'll come running for miles across the frozen marsh. He'll be hoping to find a female at this end.'

They waited but no animal appeared so he tried again. 'Of course,' he said, 'it can be dangerous. A grizzly often arrives lookin' fer his lunch.'

Fortunately most of the latter had already started to hibernate, crawling into their winter holes. Suddenly a large-nosed creature with a big spread of antlers poked his nose out of the dark forest.

'Curiosity sure killed the cat,' Scope muttered, as he took aim with the Marlin Ballard. He only needed one bullet, hitting the big bull in the side beneath the left foreleg. Somewhat stupidly the moose staggered on towards them still looking for the cow that had been calling. But it had been a heart shot and he suddenly tumbled dead in the snow.

'Good shootin',' Skookum cried, drawing his scalping knife and running forward. Both men knew it was important to skin the creature while he

180

was still warm, before he froze solid.

Scope helped butcher the body and piled it on a tarpaulin on the sled, tying it tight. 'I'll have these, too,' he said, slinging the antlers on top. 'You sure saved us some time lookin' for him, old-timer.'

'Enough of the old-timer,' Skookum grunted. 'I ain't that old.'

They took a couple of shots of the whiskey that Skookum had thoughtfully brought along before heading back. He looked out over the vast, empty terrain and asked, 'What you gonna do about Frenchie Pete? You goin' after him?'

'Nope, not until the spring, anyhow. But, don't worry, we'll meet again. There'll be a reckoning.'

He turned to Rajah and loosened the lariat from his head, patting his strong neck and muttering. 'You're free now, fella. You're on your own.' He suddenly whacked him with the rope. 'Go! Git outa here. Skedaddle!'

The gelding skittered away then

turned as if waiting for them to follow. Scope waved him away. 'Come on, Jim, let's head back.'

He whipped up the dogs and shouted to them to move, in the commands they understood, sending them heaving and straining, dragging the weighty sled back up to the ridge. Halfway up Scope called them to a halt and turned to look back. Rajah was still standing where they had left him as if wondering what to do. 'Go on,' Scope yelled. 'We'll see you in the spring.'

Skookum glanced at the young man and noticed a tear trickling from his eye. But that was maybe just the bitter cold. 'Yuh, let's go,' he grunted.

They turned their backs on the horse, both men wondering if they would see him again. 'It's best,' Scope said. 'I'd no more shoot him than I would Kai. Yeah, let's get this meat in my deep freeze.'

★　★　★

'Jeesis!' Skookum Jim exclaimed when the two weary travellers returned. 'What's been happening!'

A scene of devastation greeted them.

Scope had built a pole fence across the entrance to his mine to stable the mule inside and give it protection from the weather. It had been smashed aside and with one mighty blow of his claw the grizzly must have half torn off the terrified creature's head. The mule lay on the floor, a bloody mess. The predator had obviously a taste for mules, too.

That was not all he had fancied. He had heaved his way into the cabin, toppled chairs, ripped apart bunks and torn shelves from the walls. Apart from the mess of flour, beans and sugar on the floor, a big can of peaches Scope was keeping for a Christmas Day treat had been punctured by the creature's huge teeth and its contents sucked out.

'He's been having a fine old time,' Skookum said.

'Yeah.' Scope looked around with

dismay. 'No wonder they call him *ursus horribilis*.'

'Why ain't he gone into his hole yet? His time-clock must be wrong.'

'Waal,' Scope muttered, righting one of his log chairs, 'I guess he's reluctant to when there's all this free food about.'

The grizzly had obviously made a half-hearted effort to get into his cold store, pulling a couple of the boulders and branches away. 'Musta been sated by a meal of mule, flour and peaches,' Skookum remarked. 'He's saving the smoked salmon for another day.'

'Or night,' Scope replied, dolefully.

'Well, I'm damn glad he chose you, not me,' Jim smirked, 'It musta been quite a comical sight, him trying to git his nose in that torn peaches tin.'

'Glad you find it funny.'

'Doncha worry, I'll come back tomorrow and take a turn on guard.' Jim busied himself depositing the big joints of moose in the cold store, then they covered it up, rolling bigger boulders on top for protection. 'He's welcome to them Frenchie corpses,' he grunted, 'but he ain't having our moose.'

'Let's have a mug of coffee,' Scope said, 'an' I could do with a shot of that corn liquor in it.'

'Good idea,' Jim hooted, 'then I'd better git back an' check out *my* cabin.'

'Poor devil,' Scope mused, as he sat and supped the brew and mourned the mule. 'He wouldn't have had a chance. Still, I'd been wondering what I was going to do about him. He couldn't have fended on his own. And I've just about run outa split corn or anythang to feed him.'

'What you gonna do? Eat him?'

'No. But the dogs will. Guess I'll have to chop him up and stew him.'

'What about the moose hide?'

'I'll peg it out to dry, make some rawhide thongs of it. I need to fashion myself some snow shoes.'

'Looks like you got your work cut out, son.'

'But first I got to take care of a

185

certain character when he comes calling.'

'Grizzlies take a lot of killing, boy, specially one that size. You'll have to make sure of him pretty fast.' Skookum cackled as he got up to leave. 'Or it'll be you he makes into stew.'

★   ★   ★

Scope spent a restless night, reaching for his rifle at every creak of movement outside. He had rigged up a tripwire attached to the trigger of one of the Frenchies' revolvers which he strung to a bough of a pine hanging over his cold store. It would be unlikely to hit the bear if it went off, but it would certainly sound the alarm.

Two days passed and he busied himself breaking ice in the creek for water and tidying the cabin. He tried making laces of the dried moose hide, working in grease, but he didn't have the skill of an Indian at such work. The laces were tough and hard to use, but nonetheless he made a serviceable pair of bentwood snow shoes.

Always he kept the rifle close at hand and was alert to any sound. But he began to half-hope that with the temperature plummeting to about forty below zero the bear had become drowsy and headed for his winter slumber.

There was not a lot anyone could do at their claims now that the ground had frozen hard. Even if they could dig out a pile of earth there was no water to sluice it. A mantle of white covered the ground, icicles hung from the cabin eaves and snow globbed the pines. Some miners tried to burn holes through the snow and melt the ground and a pall of smoke hung over the creeks. But it was a thankless task. Might as well just try to stay alive and wait for the melt. Most men headed off whenever the fancy took them to cram into Belinda's joint, play cards, hang over the big potbelly stove, sozzle their brains, or frolic with the painted and padded harpies. It was a profession that aged a female fast.

So, it was pretty quiet along Eldorado and especially up there at 69 Skookum Creek. Jim, too, had decided the grizzly had gone to earth, but occasionally called up for a smoke and a chat. Lucky it was he did.

They were breaking ice in the stream one morning, looking to see through the hole to try to catch some fresh fish. They, too, seemed to go into a state of suspended animation in the winter. Suddenly, a revolver shot cracked out and the dogs set up a howl. Scope snatched up his rifle and Skookum grabbed his shotgun and they prowled up the slope to see what was going on.

There he was, trying to wreck the cold store. The tripwire gunshot had not deterred him. He was behind the cabin, but side on. Scope steadied himself, aimed and fired. At that moment the grizzly moved and roared with anger and puzzlement as he was hit in the shoulder.

He reared up on his hind legs, at least

fifteen feet tall, sniffing the air, locating Scope. And then he charged downhill at him. He must have been covering the ground at thirty miles per hour and Scope only had time to lever the rifle and snap off another shot. That one caught the bear in the belly, but he still didn't stop bounding towards him, roaring his murderous intent. There was nothing Scope could do but stand his ground, try to fire again. He was looking into the slavering jaws of death.

Skookum had run to one side. He swung round and loosed both barrels of his shotgun at the bear's fast-loping hide. The grizzly swirled around, roaring his wrath, seeking the new attacker. It gave Scope brief seconds to lever in another slug to the breech. He made no mistake, putting a bullet between the creature's eyes.

The grizzly gave another roar, then slumped forward and rolled over, dead at his feet. Scope fired twice more to make sure. 'Whoo-ee!' He let out his breath with a whistle of relief. 'I thought I was a gonner.'

'You did the right thang, kept firing,' Jim said, coming over to take a look. 'You wouldn't have had a chance if you'd run.'

'To tell the truth I didn't have time to think. It was automatic reaction.' Scope grinned and rolled the bear over. 'He's sure got a nice coat. Not one of them mangy ones. Whose is he? Mine or yours?'

'You're welcome. I ain't partial to bear meat, though my kin reckon it gives 'em strength. Some of the grease might come in handy for my lamps.'

Scope suddenly felt triumphant and punched the air. 'Well, that's another problem solved. All I gotta do now is go and see Alice. See what she's playing at.'

10

By late November, winter's fangs had really begun to bite. Alice could hardly keep on her feet as she made her way along the icy boardwalks of Dawson City. Nor, at first, did she recognize the man mushing into town a team of dogs. He wore a moose-hide cap, its earflaps tied under his chin, dark goggles against snow blindness, and his face was covered by ashes and grease, the miners' salve against razor sharp winds. He was hanging on to the back of a sled, his legs and boots protectd by leggings of caribou fur, a bandanna knotted up across his mouth and his double-breasted canvas coat buttoned tight. He had a rifle slung across his back.

'Scope . . . ?' she faltered as he slid to a halt. 'Is that you?'

Alice, too, was bundled up in her

overcoat, muffler and gloves. All Scope recognized was her pert, sweet smile beneath her big fur hat. 'It sure is,' he drawled pulling down his bandanna. 'I heard you are OK. You're looking well.'

'You, too.' Her serious grey eyes contemplated him. 'I'm glad. I've been wanting to thank you and Skookum Jim for saving my life. I'm living with Florence. Come and have some coffee. It's about all there is to be had. There are terrible shortages here.'

Scope was surprised to find Sergeant Jim MacArthur at the cabin on Front Street. He nodded to him and Florence, who was preparing a meal. 'Howdy.'

'Jim's been very kind,' Alice explained. 'He's been sharing his food with us.'

'Each officer gets a pound of bacon and a pound of flour a day,' Jim said, gruffly. 'It's more than enough for me.'

'Must get kinda monotonous,' Scope replied, as he warmed himself at the stove. 'But I guess it's more than a lot of men round here get. Most of the cheechakos up in the creeks haven't a clue how to survive. All they eat is sourdough flapjacks. Ain't no wonder their teeth are falling out and they're going down with scurvy.'

'What do tram conductors and bank clerks know about survival?' MacArthur replied, in a stern manner. 'There'll be hundreds more dead before long. We're providing three-month food packs to any who want to try hiking back to Skagway. Nine hundred have gone already but I'm not too optimistic about their chances.'

'Enough of this morbid talk,' Florence chimed in, bringing a platter to the table. 'Come along, Scope, tuck into some bacon pudding. You'll be eager to get back, no doubt, once you've concluded your business. But if you've come in for supplies I'm afraid you're out of luck.'

Scope joined them at the table and after munching through the repast and listening to some small talk about how the sun never set on Queen Victoria's empire, he butted in. 'The business I've got here ain't to get supplies. I want to talk to Alice, private-like.'

'If you've anything to say,' Florence snapped, 'you can say it in front of all of us.'

'OK.' He met the girl's grey eyes. 'It's about your share in the mine. Do you want to keep it? Or do you want to sell out to Skookum Jim?'

'I don't know,' she said, glancing at MacArthur. 'Is there any more gold in there?'

'Sure there is. There's a pile ready to wash out and come spring I'm gonna start digging that seam 'til I hit bedrock.'

'Don't you think this young lady's had enough of that life?' Florence cried. 'Surely you recall what happened to her.'

'Sure I remember. Every day. And I blame myself for leaving her at the cabin alone. By the way, Alice, I brought you a present.' He got to his feet and dug from his pack the caribou parka, leggings, fur boots and mittens. 'Got these from the Indians. They'll keep you warmer than that overcoat of yourn.'

'I'm very grateful, Scope.' Alice stood to look at the clothes. 'It's good of you.'

'Put it all on, gal.'

'What now?' She smiled with surprise. 'Why?'

'Because you're coming with me.'

'Don't be ridiculous,' Florence shrieked. 'Do you think a well-bred young lady like Alice wants to spend six months alone with you in a backwoods cabin? Absurd.'

'That's up to her? How about it, gal?'

'Hold on, young man, you can't just come barging in here.' MacArthur stood up, too, neatly-uniformed, his chevrons of rank on his scarlet coat. 'It so happens I have an interest in Alice's welfare.'

'I bet you have and I don't blame you, pal. So, she's gonna have to choose. You, or me?'

'There's no contest,' Florence snorted.

'Jim's solid, dependable. There's talk of him being made commissioner. What can you offer? You're just some back-woods rat.'

'Please, Florence,' Alice protested, 'don't say things like that.'

'And don't you keep looking at my rifle, MacArthur. Sure, I ain't paid your tax.' Scope pulled out a pouch of gold dust. 'How much do I owe?'

'We'll discuss that some other time.'

'Yeah, all you Limeys think about is taxing this and licensing that. You oughta come and live in the country of the free sometime.'

'Free, huh? Are your Indians free? What's left of them. However, the point is, Mitchell, I'm not allowing you to force this young woman to throw in her lot with you. Her health is not good, she — '

'I'm sorry, Jim. You've been good.' Alice had pulled on the bulky parka over her blouse and jersey. 'I feel like an Indian now! Can you give me time to pack my things, Scope?'

The young American grinned at her. 'All you need is some underwear and your toothbrush, gal.'

Florence was still protesting when he tucked the bearskin, still with its head and claws, about Alice as she sat on the sled. 'Goodbye, Florence.' The girl smiled, radiantly, and waved as Scope set the dogs in motion and they went skimming away. 'Goodbye, Jim. Thank you.'

'Some gratitude, after all we've done for her,' Florence sulked. 'The silly young fool.' MacArthur simply shook his head, sadly, and watched them go.

★　★　★

Alice was so numb with cold by the time they reached the cabin Scope had to pick her up and carry her bodily inside. He gently laid her down on her bed, took off her mittens and massaged her hands, before getting a blaze going in the tin stove.

Alice looked about her, wonderingly,

in the candlelight, trying to control the shivers that racked her body. Flashing back into her mind came the ghastly memories: Couteau, his chain, his knife, biting, thrusting at her like an animal. No, that was an insult to animals, they at least showed some respect towards their mates. 'I'm so lucky,' she murmured, 'I didn't have his child.'

Scope knelt down beside her, wiped the bear-grease from her cheeks. 'That's over now.'

'It will never be over. That other man. He came through that door. I shot him, Scope. I killed him.'

'You had to. They would have killed you.' He undid the parka and eased out her arms. 'You gotta live with it, Alice. You gotta go on with life.'

'I guess so.' She was feeling warmer now and took the pins from her luxuriant black hair, shaking it out to her shoulders. 'I'm glad I came back, Scope.'

He was about to rise, to attend to the

pan of moose head stew that had begun to bubble on the stove, when she caught hold of him, her arms around his neck, her eyes smiling. 'Don't go, Scope.'

'I don't intend to,' he murmured as he bent forward and touched her moist, warm lips with his own. 'Not ever, Alice. It's just you and me now.'

'No,' she murmured, pulling him into her and kissing him hard. 'It's me and you! It's us.'

★ ★ ★

It was the unearthly silence, the darkness, the howling of the wolves, the shrieks of frozen trees suddenly splitting apart, the absence of sunlight, the intense cold that choked breath from the lungs, that unnerved most Yukoners. Not just the starvation diet of flour and water, the sickness and melancholy it induced. Men cut off by blizzards, cooped up in their small cabins for months on end, went out of their minds, crazy with shack fever. Others drank themselves to death.

At times the temperature fell to 60° below on the Fahrenheit scale. Desperate, the poet, Joaquin Miller, tried to walk out from Dawson to Circle City. He crawled back on his hands and knees, was nursed by the Sisters of Anne, but lost forever an ear and toes. Others were not so lucky. Tales of men stewing their boots for sustenance were not exaggerated. They reckoned it took eight hours stewing to make them tender enough to chew.

By comparison Scope and Alice were comfortable. They kept warm, lived on salmon, moose meat, roots and berries — for their anti-scorbutic properties — and ventured out on the sled when the few twilight hours allowed. They even made a trip with Skookum Jim to visit his relatives and Scope stocked up with Indian tobacco. In the evenings, Alice would read to him from her copy of *Pickwick Papers*. Or, more often, they would strip naked and make love beneath the bearskin. It was odd how one forgot about the brittle cold when one was having sex.

At least, that was what Alice thought. There seemed to be so many variations of their bodies' interlocking to explore. They hardly noticed time go by. One night Alice murmured, 'Who needs the sun? This is my sun rising.'

Scope gulped as her mouth enclosed him. 'You certainly know a few tricks, gal.'

But Alice was unable to reply. She had visited India once with her father and seen some strange carvings on a temple. Never in her wildest dreams had she thought she, too, would be practising such arts!

The dark days lasted until March when men rejoiced to see the sun's brief hovering on the horizon. It brought no real warmth until May, but gradually the creeks began to gurgle again. There was no longer any need to break through six feet of ice to drink.

Ever hopeful, work began at the claims. With the melt the extent of the disaster was apparent as corpses were washed down the creeks and into the broken ice of the Yukon. But why worry about the dead?

'Yukon or bust', was still the cry.

When Scope climbed back across the divide he was not really expecting to find Rajah alive. But there he was, grazing amid some caribou on a snowfree slope. A sharp whistle and he came trotting across to take the offered sugar lumps. He rode him without a saddle to the cabin.

Now work could truly start on hauling more clay from their mine, sieving it in the rocker Scope had built, washed in water guided in flumes from the stream. The gold sparkled in the sunlight and each day their take increased. It was a backbreaking occupation, but they were getting good reward. The bonanza finds were few and far between. But most prospectors got a reasonable return, although there were many who found nothing at all.

★   ★   ★

'What wouldn't I give to soak in a deep tub?' Alice sighed when in mid-June Scope announced his intention of taking their haul into town to see what it was worth. 'I'd give a thousand dollars' worth of dust, at least.'

'You may have to,' Scope replied, as he saddled Rajah, 'From what I've heard.'

In the dark months Alice had tried bathing in a pan on the floor, but it was so cold the boiling water from the stove would start to freeze before she hardly had a chance to lower herself in. She had taken, instead, to nipping out naked from the cabin and rolling in a snowdrift before running in to towel herself dry vigorously.

But, as they set off, two-up on Rajah, towing the gold on the Indian sled, watched by the dogs they had left in the care of Skookum Jim, she turned and looked back at the cabin. A pang of regret at leaving it jagged through her. Cold, dark and difficult as it was, it had been their world.

★   ★   ★

Dawson was a different kettle of fish. The mosquitoes, the flies, the stench, the crowds. It was like returning from living on the moon, back to the real world. It took some getting used to. When the ice melted, 500 skows and rafts had set off down the rapids to the gold capital. The steamship companies had got organized and more stern-wheelers were coming through loaded with passengers.

'The population has swollen to 30,000,' Jim MacArthur told them. 'And still they keep coming.'

Florence had made a pile buying and selling, had got a stupendous $20,000 for her lot on Front Street and was preparing to go home.

A man on a ladder was already painting a new name above the big sign outside her cabin which announced 'Gold Bought and Sold'. She had agreed to vacate in four days. The front of her cabin had been set aside as an assayer's office. Florence weighed their sacks of gold and examined it. 'This is top quality,' she announced. 'I could get you a much better price in San Francisco than you could get here.'

Scope looked a tad worried. Could they trust her? Alice smiled encouragingly. Florence might be a little odd but she was honest. 'I could send you a cheque for what I get to the Bank of Seattle,' the New York woman drawled. 'Minus my commission, of course.'

'Sounds fine to me,' Scope agreed, offering his hand to shake on the deal. 'All I need's some spending money while we're in town.'

He turned to Jim MacArthur. 'Have you caught up with that scumbag, Frenchie Pete, yet?'

'Hear tell he's back in Skagway,' the sergeant replied. 'We can't touch him. There's no extradition agreement, no law in Alaska.'

'Maybe it's time a man made his own law,' Scope muttered.

Outside in the hurly burly of the street, Alice hung on tight to him. 'It sounds as if America's at war with Spain,' she shouted through the din. Men were queuing outside a tent, eager to pay ten dollars to hear a man read from a a news-sheet that had just arrived, the only copy in town, about how the battleship *Maine* had been sunk.

'I ain't queueing to hear that,' Scope said. 'It'll be in all the rags tomorrow. We're rich. It's time to enjoy ourselves.'

★ ★ ★

Big business had arrived in Dawson City. The Bank of Canada had started in a tent but now had a three-storey block where Scope traded their remaining dust for $10,000. There were offices of lawyers, assayers, investment companies, jostling for space on Front Street. Amid the bustling throng two sisters, Pollie and Lottie Oatley, were singing and clog-dancing on the sidewalk, a tin can for contributions before them. When they later opened their show in a cabin they made $5,000 a week. An opera house had gone up advertizing 'The Nightingale of the North'. Every third establishment was a saloon or beer parlour. And men queued around the clock in Paradise Alley outside the red-curtained cabins of prostitutes young and old. The miners had given a big send-off to one popular teenager, Myrtle Brocée, who, unable to bear the life any longer, shot herself. But most of the women would go home with $20,000 in their belts.

A hot bath didn't cost Alice $1,000, but a room in one of the best hotels, aptly named the Nugget, for three days did. A bowl of fresh fruit from the newly annexed Sandwich Isles, renamed Hawaii, was a marvel to the senses, as were the freshly laundered sheets.

'We can afford it, gal,' Scope said, as they stretched out beneath the mosquito net. 'Not that I'm planning to throw my cash away. Too many men have made that mistake.'

Of course, they weren't in the same league as Swede Charlie Anderson, who had at first regretted his drunken bid but took out $230,000; the Berrys, who had returned that summer to their mine to reap in all $250,000, and sold out for $2 million; a miner called Bruceth who struck $60,000 of gold in one day's digging on the Eldorado; or McDonald who made $7 million and had just refused $150,000 for his plot on the same gulch. But there wasn't a man on the Eldorado who hadn't made $10,000 that summer and they were spending it liberally.

Scope and Alice spent an exhausting three days seeing the sights, going in and out of the saloons and dance halls, buying all and everybody drinks. They took a private box for a performance of *Camille* at the opera house with champagne provided at $40 a quart.

But there were less salubrious sights, bear and dog fights, circus freaks, wrestling matches, and a macabre act in a hall where each night a man was hanged, dropping through a trap, going red in the face as he choked, before the curtains were drawn. A different deadbeat took the job every night so nobody knew whether he lived or died.

In the Monte Carlo fortunes were being won or lost at roulette and blackjack every night. Swiftwater Bill had fallen crazily in love with Gorgeous Gussie and offered her her weight in gold to marry him. Gussie took the gold but still refused. Their violent fights were legendary. Bill was in despair as he watched Gussie waltzing around with another beau.

'I'm going to show her,' he said, as he rolled his dark eyes and stroked his black beard. 'I've bought the only consignment of eggs to reach Dawson. Gussie's expecting to get a platter served up in the morning. She's in for a surprise.'

Scope wasn't a gambling man so they didn't stay to see the fun. But they heard next day that when Gussie ordered her breakfast platter, Swiftwater ignored her, whistled up all the dogs in town and fed them fried eggs from his restaurant one by one. The two crates of eggs had cost him $2,000 and Gorgeous Gussie gave him a black eye for his pains!

By the third night, when they got back to their hotel, Scope was beginning to feel jaded by the constant round of pleasure, the sight of all the sin and squalor. 'It's time we got back to Gold Hill, gal, and see how much more we can git outa there.'

Alice did not tell him she would not be going back with him. That night their lovemaking was imbued with a bitter-sweet wildness and abandon. Alice clung desperately to him with feverish kisses. This might be the last night they would ever be together.

In the morning, after breakfast, dressed in her new city costume, her face serious, she told him. 'I'm leaving, Scope. I'm going with Florence. She's booked me passage to San Francisco. I've got to get back to New York.'

It hit him hard. He drank his coffee in silence for a while and finally asked, 'Why?'

'I haven't told you. I'm too ashamed to speak of it. My father is in prison. Debtor's prison. My mother and sister are living in acute poverty. I've got enough now with my share to get him out, set them up in a decent house of their own.'

'You sayin' you won't be coming back?'

'I don't know. I'll have to see.' She wanted to return to his arms. But she blinked back tears and turned away. 'I must go. Florence will be waiting.'

'Yeah,' he said, bitterly. 'She's more your sort than me.'

'Don't be like that, Scope. Don't make it harder for me.'

He watched the two 'society ladies' drag Florence's big cabin trunk up the gangplank of a three-storey stern-wheeler, the SS *Monarch*. The trunk was packed with gold dust, mostly his. Silently, he watched as the ropes were cast off, the paddles churned, the steam siren boomed, and the ship moved out towards the wide Yukon to head north and the freedom of the open sea. He watched as the young woman fluttering her 'kerchief became an indistinct speck and all that could be seen were the twin tall stacks drifting smoke.

Scope pulled his coat back and patted the gutta-percha butt of the Iver Johnson on his hip. He strode towards the livery to collect Rajah, then consulted steamship timetables. 'Gimme a ticket on the next ship to Skagway,' he said.

11

Soapy Smith had ordered a new white Stetson all the way from Texas and proudly wore it with his pearl-grey suit and fancy high-heel boots as he strolled around. Business boomed as more and more cheechakos arrived to try their luck. The population of Skagway City had soared to 20,000 with hundreds of false-front frame buildings, supplemented by thousands of log cabins and tents.

To display his patriotism and support for the far-off war in Cuba, he had formed his thugs into a company of infantry he termed the Skagway Guards and, seated on a prancing pony, led them through the city for a fourth of July parade. He distributed bags of candy and peanuts to every child, organized firecrackers, dynamite explosions and a grand rocket display, which added to the tumult and rode back to his saloon as the town band played 'Yankee Doodle Dandy'.

Everybody had a grand time, but to many honest traders of Skagway, Smith's bid for self-gratification had a hollow ring. Too many had been fleeced by Soapy's gang. By now a district judge and a US marshal had been appointed to try to bring some law and order to Alaska. But, with the backing of only three US marines they appeared ineffectual. The citizens had had enough of cheating and thuggery and three days after the Fourth a vigilante committee was formed. Now rival bodies of armed men prowled the streets, like bristling mongrel dogs, in an uneasy truce.

'Nobody's gonna run me outa town,' the saloon-keeper bragged as he held centre of attention in Jeff's Place. But even he could see that maybe it was time to gather his assets in case of the need for a hasty departure.

When Frenchie Pete had turned up

with sacks of stolen gold dust worth $20,000 he had persuaded him to invest it in the gaming house and become an 'equal partner'. Pete had readily agreed.

'All the others dead, huh?' Jeff muttered. 'What happened to Scope Mitchell.'

'We put a bullet in his leg.' Pete bragged. 'He won't bother us no more.'

Soapy wasn't so sure. Maybe that was another reason to be ready to quit the sinking ship.

By now an aerial cable lift had been constructed to transport equipment and baggage to the top of the Chilcoot Pass. Smith had not been slow to see it was a profitable operation and had sent his heavies to demand a share, or else.

'I got a job for you, Frenchie,' Smith drawled that day. 'I want you to go to the top of the pass and collect what we're owed. It should be quite a wad.'

Frenchie was comfortable at the bar and shook his shaggy head, glowering across. 'Why me?'

'Because you're the only one I can trust. You don't want us to miss out, do you?'

Frenchie finished his drink and headed for the door. 'I'll be back soon,' he called to a gal called Big Sal he had been planning on having.

When he reached the machine-room at the foot of the pass he was told he would have to see the manager up at the top. To save time Frenchie insisted, at revolver point, on being carried up in one of the lift buckets rather than have to join the queue slowly climbing up the pass on foot. It was a precarious ride as the bucket swung from the moving steel wire suspended from support trestles. But it didn't take long. Frenchie whooped with triumph when he reached the top. 'Hey, you mugs,' he shouted. 'Where's the boss?'

* * *

Scope Mitchell had paid $175 for a berth on the SS *Bellingham*, a 100-ton boat, the first to ply the route from Dawson City all the way up river to Lake Bennett. Smaller than the other steamers it was otherwise identical, a sternwheeler with three tiers of cabins and tall stacks. Its shallow draught and powerful wood-burning engine made it possible to push through the rapids and strong currents, its siren booming to warn raftsmen speeding through.

'Sure beats walking, don't it?' Scope remarked when he led Rajah off the boat as it berthed at Lake Bennett. Now there were only forty miles left to ride.

He covered that through the short summer night and it must have been high noon when he traversed the glacier and reached the mountie post at the top of the pass. He arranged to leave Rajah in their care rather than pay any extra export tax and, carrying his rifle slung over his back, went on on foot.

It was one of those odd coincidences that when he spotted the new cabin housing the machinery operating the aerial lift from the top, who should step from the doorway but Frenchie Pete. He was stuffing a wad of cash into his pocket when he heard Scope shout.

'Hey, you thievin', murderin' rat,' the young American yelled. 'I want a word with you.'

Frenchie looked around with surprise, shaking his black hair from out of his eyes, the white scar across his cheek vivid in the sunshine. '*Merde*,' he muttered, dragging his .45 from his belt. 'Where you come from?' He loosed two shots at Scope and turned to run towards the lift. He climbed hastily into one of the empty tubs that was clanking on its way back down to the foot of the pass.

Scope's instinct was to run after him. He covered the forty yards over slippery mud as fast as he could and clambered into an empty iron bucket that was just moving away. 'Jesus!' he cried as he went swinging out into space. He had to hang on tight with both hands until he had acclimatized himself to the ride.

Twang! A bullet bounced off the bucket's side reminding him what he was there for. He hung on with his left hand and drew the Iver Johnson with his right. Frenchie was in the next bucket some forty feet away, blamming away with the Colt. Scope aimed at the fire flash but it was not easy for both iron buckets swung wildly back and forth as they trundled down the descent. Three carefully aimed shots from the triple action all missed the scowling thug. He ducked down as Frenchie's last three slugs whined past his head.

Maybe, Scope thought, he could take him out with the rifle. But he didn't want to kill him, at least, not before he found out what he had done with his dust. Pete had obviously run out of bullets and was desperately trying to reload. The Iver Johnson, too, was empty so Scope thrust it back in his holster.

By now they were about a third of the way down, the wire suspended high in space by the pine trestleworks. Scope's heart lurched as the bucket swayed, but a madness of vengeance made him clamber from the bucket and leap out to grab the wire in his gloved hands.

'You crazy bastard,' Frenchie yelled as he saw the American swinging his way towards him hand over hand, a grim look on his clean-shaven face. The Frenchman had found some slugs in his coat pocket but fumbled as he panicked and half-watched his adversary sliding and swinging along the wire. He failed to insert the bullets into the cylinder and hurled the heavy revolver at Scope as he swung up his boots and tried to climb into the tub.

The gun hit Scope hard in the throat, spinning away, making him almost lose his grip. But a lucky kick to Pete's chin knocked him back. Gathering all his strength, Scope hauled himself over the edge of the iron bucket as Frenchie scrambled to his feet.

Scope hit him with a straight right to the chest, but he was no pushover.

Hard as nails in fact, as he replied with a piledriver to the American's head. Both men were swapping blows as the iron bucket creaked sickeningly from side to side.

A jab from a sneaky left to the solar plexus made Frenchie gasp and double up and Scope had him by the throat, cracking his skull back against the bucket edge. Dazed and half out of it, Pete croaked as Scope's iron grip closed about his throat and he half-choked him.

'What you done with my gold, you scumbag!' Scope gritted out. 'You'd better cough it out, or — '

'Soapy's got it,' Frenchie gasped, as the grip tightened. 'I give it him.'

'Right! That better be true.' The American hauled him to his feet. 'I'm arrestin' you and takin' you back. The mounties'll deal with you.'

Frenchie made a desperate effort to break free, swinging his fist to thud into Scope's temple. Scope pushed him away. The bucket lurched, almost overturned and Pete was hurled out. Scope hung on and saw the Frenchman crack his head against a trestle post and go hurtling to the rocks below. When he looked back he was lying still, blood pouring from his skull.

'That louse got what he deserved,' he muttered, as the bucket clattered on its way and he climbed from it at the foot of the descent. He pushed through the workmen who had been watching the fight and headed on along the trail. He had a date at Jeff's Place.

★　★　★

Skagway was smouldering like a fuse to a powder keg. The tension was at breaking point as Jeff Soapy Smith lined up his gang of thugs, guns at the ready, across the boardwalk entrance to Jeff's Place. The vigilante committee, rifles at hand, had retreated across the wide main street, taking up positions for battle. Meanwhile, a seething mob were being stirred up by blacksmith

Kurt Schwimmer, who had a stout rope and noose in his fists. 'I'll string him from the rafter in my barn,' he shouted angrily, for he, too, had been a victim of Smith's extortion.

'Burn him down,' a woman in the mob screamed.

Such was the state of affairs when Scope, who had hitched a lift on a wagon, arrived. He stepped down outside Jeff's Place and wondered just how he was going to get inside.

United States Marshal was scrawled on a sign above a cabin nearby. 'Maybe I'd better try lawful means first,' he muttered.

'What can I do?' the marshal, Henry Tremayne, replied when he heard his complaint.

Another miner, Frank Reid, was already in his office protesting that he had been robbed of his poke of $2,500 in dust by Smith's bully boys the previous night.

'You'll both have to bring your actions in a court and prove your accusations,' Tremayne told them. 'That won't be easy.'

'To hell with that. I'm gonna git my dust back whether you git off your ass or not,' Reid shouted. 'I've worked damn hard for it. It's all I got.'

'I wouldn't advise that.' Tremayne tried to calm them both down. 'You two stay here. I'll go over and see if Jeff's willing to pay you back.'

Scope wondered if the marshal, too, might be in Soapy's pocket, but he guessed he had an unenviable job to do. He stood and watched as the marshal went over to Jeff's Place and pushed through the bunch of gun-toting men. He wasn't in there long.

'Mr Smith says he has no idea what either of you are talking about,' Tremayne told them when he returned. 'So I advise you two gentlemen — '

'You can advise all you like, mister,' Reid snarled, 'but I ain't aiming to let that skunk git away with this.'

Rumour had got around that Soapy

was planning to leave town and the vigilante committee and the rest of the mob backed away down to the pier to take a stance to make sure that he and his thugs did not escape.

It was, indeed, true, and Smith had emptied his safe and stuffed wads of dollars, coins, gems, and pouches of gold dust, worth about $100,000 into a big velvet carpet bag. His wallet and pockets were bulging, too, as he grabbed his Winchester and headed towards the door.

'Come on, boys,' he growled to the dozen gunmen who had stuck by him. 'We're takin' a vacation. There's no way they're gonna stop us.'

Many of his tough-guy hangers-on had drifted away, hiding out in other saloons, not wanting to get involved now the chips were down. Even the big Norwegian, Lars Lanson, looked uneasy. 'Where you gonna go, boss?' he asked.

'San Francisco. Where else? C'mon, the *Excelsior*'s getting up steam. We got no time to lose. I got a fortune in here.' He patted the carpet bag. 'All you boys got to do is get us through to the pier. Nobody's gonna argue. They ain't got the guts. Y'all git your share of this.'

The SS *Excelsior* was blowing her whistle, eager to depart, as Smith emerged from the saloon in his white Stetson, and flanked by his men, headed down towards the beach and the wooden jetty. The vigilantes and the lynch mob stood silently awaiting him, but he was confident they wouldn't want bloodshed.

'That's far enough.' Reid's voice rang out behind him. 'You owe me, Soapy.'

Jeff Smith, in his long black fox fur, was walking behind his line of body-guards. He swivelled around and raised his Winchester, threateningly, after carefully placing the carpet bag on the ground. 'Don't shoot, Reid,' he whined, 'I'm begging you.'

But the miner, incensed, raised his revolver. When he pulled the trigger, however, it misfired. Smith didn't hesitate. He squeezed out a shot, snarling, 'You damn fool!' Hit in the chest, Reid was bowled over to sprawl back in the mud, blood pouring from his wound.

'How about me, Soapy?' Scope called.

Smith blinked with surprise at the avenging young American. He levered the Winchester and fired. 'Go to hell!'

Scope stepped aside, aimed from the hip with the Ballard. The bullet took off the top of the saloon-keep's head and he stumbled back and lay prostrate.

The line of thugs had turned, guns ready to fire, but lost their nerve when they saw the young American facing them, steadfastly. 'It ain't worth the trouble, boys,' Scope shouted. 'Your paymaster's dead.'

★   ★   ★

If they had had their way the lynch mob would have strung up all of Soapy's boys. But the US marshal, Tremayne, arrived with his three marines and pacified them. 'We'll round 'em all up, folks,' he said, 'don't you worry. We'll ship 'em back to the States to serve their time.'

Scope hung around long enough for the judge to make an official enquiry. He was awarded the $20,000 he claimed was his out of Smith's carpet bag. What happened to the rest was anybody's guess.

He pushed out of the court through the throng, many of whom wanted to buy him a drink or three. 'I ain't got time,' he said, shouldering his rifle and setting off towards the Chilcoot Pass. 'I gotta git back to my mine.'

The miner Reid had died of his wounds. 'He shoulda kept his gun oiled,' Scope muttered. 'You can never be too careful in this country.'

12

Scope worked on through the long lonely winter into the next summer. By then big investors like Daniel Guggen-heim, the billionaire, had moved in on the Yukon believing they had found the mother lode, that the gold fields would prove to be the richest in the world. A railroad had been built to White Horse by the summer of '99. The Golden Triangle resounded to thudding of steam hammers, diggers, drills and power hoses. Maybe the Yukon was not the biggest but it certainly made millionaires of poor men. Never before had it been so easy to dig gold from the *placers* — a Spanish word indicating a pleasant place. But as soon as they were scraped clean there was little room in the gold fields for the little man.

'I'm packing up,' Skookum Jim told Scope one morning. 'Thar's a new stampede on up to a place called Nome on the north coast. You comin', friend?'

'What you gonna do with all your gold?'

'Aw, I've hid it in a hole up in the hills. It might come in handy for my old age. Dawson's gittin' too damn civilized, anyhow. They got seven churches now and ladies' committees of temperance. Yuk!'

Scope grinned at the older man, who, in his concertina'd top hat and ancient overcoat was loading a packjack with his shovel, pick and pan. It wasn't just the gold, it was the call of the wild, the unknown, that lured him on.

'Nope,' he said. 'I got enough. I'm going home.'

'I'll give you a thousand dollars for your dogs.'

'Nope. I'll be needin' 'em. We get some purty deep snow in Washington State.' He stuck out his hand. 'So long, Jim. You've been a good pal.'

The lonesome cabins on the creeks were quickly deserted. There was standing room only on the boats out of Dawson winding north along the river to the sea. Five thousand men bought tickets the first week. Scope, however, paid $1,000 for a cabin all the way to Seattle.

★   ★   ★

Two weeks later he hitched Rajah to the rail outside the general store at Skykomish, told Kai to stay with the team, and heard the familiar ding of the bell as he pushed through the door. 'Howdy, Maud,' he shouted. 'I'm back.'

'Goodness gracious!' She came from the kitchen wiping her hands on her apron as he swept her up in his arms and twirled her around. 'Is it really you?'

'Sure is.' He put her down and took a pouch from the pocket of his canvas coat. 'That's for you.'

Maud poured the glittering gold dust out on to her palm, her eyes wide. 'All this?'

'That's nuthin'.' He took an envelope from his inside pocket. 'This here's a cheque for you. Your half.'

Maud's blue eyes opened even wider as she studied the Wells Fargo cheque with its stagecoach design. 'Two hundred thousand dollars![1] Are you joking?'

'Nope. That was the deal. I wouldn't have got nuthin' if you hadn't grubstaked me. I sold out Gold Hill to the big boys for one hundred thou. It sure made another long lonesome winter worthwhile.'

'Lawks: I don't want all this.' Maud was flustered. 'What am I going to do with it all?'

'Take a trip to New York, London, Paris. Live like a duchess. You're never too old to enjoy yourself, Maud.'

'Where are you going, Scope?'

'Back up to my cabin. I'm going to build the biggest, most luxurious lodge

---

[1] The approximate value in today's currency would be $4 million.

ever seen. Dudes'll come hunt from all over the States.' He grinned at her. 'I ain't gonna work *too* hard.'

Maud stared at the cheque with disbelief. When she looked out of the window Scope had swung into the saddle and was heading up into the woods. 'But, I meant to tell you,' she stuttered. 'In all this excitement I clean forgot.'

There was a curl of blue woodsmoke drifting from the cabin chimney into the late summer sky. 'That's funny,' he said. 'Somebody's made 'emselves at home.'

Whoever it was must have heard the whinny of the horse for the door opened and she stood there.

'Alice?' He swallowed his surprise as he regarded the slim figure in her modest blue gown. 'I thought you were in New York.'

'Come on in,' she smiled. 'Supper's on the stove.'

He felt awkward as he stepped inside, almost shy, not having seen her for so long. 'Shush,' she whispered, putting a finger to her lips. 'He's asleep.'

Scope put his rifle carefully aside and bent over the cradle to study the child, who was blissfully at ease.

'Who's this?'

'It's Michael, your son. Do you think the name suits him?'

'Sure.' He gently touched the child's soft cheek with his finger. 'Miraculous, ain't it? A real boy. Mike Mitchell. Yeah, sounds good.'

He threaded his fingers into hers, pulling her into him, losing himself in her sparkling grey eyes. 'It would be nice if we could give him a li'l sister one day.'

'Well, that rabbit stew won't be ready for an hour,' she whispered. 'We could try.'